"Don't You  Touchi

He froze. "Josie, I can explain."

"Lucas told me you didn't approve of me. You came here to get rid of me, didn't you? That's why you watched me, why you slept with me. All you ever wanted to do was to make me feel cheap and bad and ruin things for Lucas and me. Well, you succeeded."

"No! I would have left you alone last night. But you had to come back out and kiss me. You seduced me."

"So this is all my fault? I hate you!"

"Right. That's why you made love to me all night long." Adam flung his card on the table. "If you change your mind after you calm down, you've got all my numbers. Call me."

Dear Reader,

This book was inspired by a personal experience that happened to me many years ago. I was shopping in an office-supply store with my three small children, and my gaze met a stranger's. Instantly, I began to shake. I had the strangest feeling that I had known him for thousands of years.

Who was he? I did not pursue the answer, but I have never forgotten that moment and I have always wondered.

Have you ever met a person who brings out an entirely new you? A forbidden you? Did you go with it or run from it?

This book is about a man and a woman who want to be ideal versions of themselves, but when they meet each other, suddenly they are naked, needy souls, who desire all that they have denied themselves. Do they risk all? Or run?

Enjoy,

Ann Major

ANN MAJOR

SOLD INTO MARRIAGE

Silhouette®

Desire

Published by Silhouette Books
America's Publisher of Contemporary Romance

 SILHOUETTE BOOKS

ISBN-13: 978-0-373-76832-5
ISBN-10: 0-373-76832-X

SOLD INTO MARRIAGE

ANN MAJOR

lives in Texas with her husband of many years and is the mother of three grown children. She has a master's degree from Texas A&M at Kingsville, Texas, and is a former English teacher. She is a founding board member of the Romance Writers of America and a frequent speaker at writers' groups.

Ann loves to write; she considers her ability to do so a gift. Her hobbies include hiking in the mountains, sailing, ocean kayaking, traveling and playing the piano. But most of all she enjoys her family.

This book is dedicated to my mother.

ACKNOWLEDGMENTS

I must thank the Silhouette Desire team
for the fabulous editorial input.

One

Her footsteps echoing like hollow heartbeats in the biting cold, Josie Navarre raced up the four flights of stone stairs that led to her Parisian apartment on the Rue du Cardinal Lemoine.

She was in a hurry to get home. Maybe to eat the food she'd just bought. Or maybe because she didn't want anybody to guess she was all alone on Christmas Eve. As if anybody in the city really knew her or cared, now that dear, sweet Lucas had gone back to Texas for the holidays.

Josie pulled out her key and refused to think about all the houses in the city overflowing with children, families, gifts, music and food because it was Christmas Eve. She refused to think about her mother and her half brothers, who wouldn't let her come home to New Orleans.

"Not even for a few days at Christmas?" she'd pleaded. Not that she was really ready to face them.

"Not even." Armand, her older brother, was maddeningly bossy. "Besides, what about Brianna's gallery?"

As luck would have it, Brianna, her dearest and oldest friend, had needed someone to look after her apartment and gallery in Paris while she was away honeymooning, and at the exact same time when Josie had gotten into trouble and had needed to get out of New Orleans fast.

"Brianna told me I should close up for the holidays," Josie had informed her brother.

"Stay there! Paint! And stay out of trouble."

"What's so special about Christmas?" Josie now said aloud to the dull, gray walls that Madame Picard, her landlady, refused to let her repaint. "Count your blessings. You have the night off. And the next two weeks. Armand's right. Paint!"

She paused outside her doorway for a moment. As always she'd avoided the claustrophobic Métro at rush hour and the equally terrifying, cagelike elevator in her building that made the kind of weird, groaning sounds one associates with dying appliances. As a result, she was breathless from the long snowy walk from the gallery and the four-story hike to her apartment. Her scarf came loose, and clouds of steamy air burst from her lips as she jiggled the key in Brianna's lock.

When Brianna's heavy door stuck, Josie kicked it with so much force the thick slab of wood crashed against the wall and sent her tumbling across the threshold. She landed on her knees, her paper sack containing her dinner flying out of her hands.

Slamming the door, she marched to the tall window that

faced the courtyard. It was dark and quiet. Madame Picard, who had a fondness for wine, garlic, her grandchildren and gossip, had told her that all her tenants were going somewhere special for the holidays.

"All except you, mademoiselle. I do have one new arrival. As soon as he checks in, I'm off to Rouen to see Remi, my grandson."

Remi was five and full of mischief. According to the doting Madame Picard, the boy had her eyes.

Since no lights were on in the other apartments that faced the courtyard, Josie didn't worry about Madame Picard's new arrival or lower her shade.

Paris had short, gray days and long, black nights in the winter. Not that the light, especially the misty, hazy morning light, wasn't wonderful. Every morning as soon as the sun rose, Josie ran to her windows and opened her shades so that she could admire the stark, leafless trees that seemed so naked and honest against the slate-gray skies.

Picking up her sack, she tugged the chain on her lamp and then switched on the little red Christmas lights she'd strung over a tiny potted ivy. When she glanced at the single envelope containing a Christmas card, note and check from her mother—her only gift beneath her diminutive, makeshift Christmas tree—a rush of guilt and homesickness swept over her.

"Our tastes are so different I never know what to get you, dear. Money is the perfect gift," her mother had written.

For people who don't really know each other. Or care.

Josie set her now damp sack that contained her *café noir,* warm brioche, yogurt and blackberries next to her laptop. On a plate beside the sofa.

She was peeking inside the sack to see how much the coffee and yogurt had leaked when the message light on her answering machine blinked madly. At the sound of Lucas Ryder's deep drawl, she jabbed the appropriate button.

"Merry Christmas! I miss you so much." Lucas's voice was pure Texas. "I told everybody about you," he said. "I showed them snapshots of your paintings. They love your wonderful gargoyles. They're all very happy for me."

His tenderness both warmed her and alarmed her. They'd met at an art opening. They hadn't known each other long but Lucas had fallen fast and hard.

"Except for my older brother." Lucas's voice sounded tense. "He doesn't get contemporary art. Or your gargoyles. He says they look like large rats."

Rats? Self-doubt, that constant demon that lurked in the depths of her artistic soul, ate a little piece out of her.

"Call me, why don't you?" Lucas left a number.

Smiling, she ripped the paper sack open and began eating her blueberries.

One by one, she slipped the berries in between her teeth and bit down on them, nibbling until they burst, sweet and tart, at the back of her throat. Licking her lips, she went to her tiny fridge and splashed Merlot into a long-stemmed glass.

She wasn't lonely or homesick! That wasn't why she replayed Lucas's message.

Again Lucas sounded as adorably Texan as he had three days ago when she'd seen him off at the Métro stop on his way to the airport. As always he'd worn boots, overly long, creased jeans and a cowboy hat.

"I'm going to tell my family all about you."

"Not that there's anything to tell."

"Yet." He'd removed a tan leather glove, emblazoned with a big black, swirling *R,* the family brand he'd told her about

with more than a little pride. He'd pulled her wool scarf down and touched the rosy tip of her frozen nose with a warm fingertip. "Some day soon I'll have a lot to tell them. I'll wait. Until you're ready."

When would that be? Would she ever get over Barnardo's awful betrayal?

"It's just that after…Barnardo…and his awful video show…" She stopped, saying only, "I—I promised my family I wouldn't date for a while."

"Your family would love me. I'm a Ryder."

"You say your name as if you think you're royalty."

"In Texas, we are. Why do you think I can afford to live in Paris on the same block where Hem lived and wrote like he did?"

Lucas had told her that before Ernest Hemingway became famous, he had lived on the Rue du Cardinal Lemoine with a young wife and child. Like Hemingway, Lucas was optimistically determined to live abroad and write great American novels that defined male machismo.

She smiled indulgently. Lucas felt as sure of himself as both her big brothers did. What would it be like to grow up feeling secure and safe?

She sipped her wine and fought not to think about a listing barge in a lost bayou and the ramshackle, shotgun house on top of it. Or the illiterate girl who'd lived there until she was thirteen.

She held her wineglass up and made a silent toast to Lucas and to the sweet love he'd professed. How different he was than Barnardo. Frowning, she forced herself to make a second toast to her own family. Someday, somehow, she would find a way to make them proud of her.

Lucas. She closed her eyes, thinking of what it might be like if they were together. She pictured his hands, his lips, and tried to imagine lying in his arms. And then his image blurred into that of a dream lover, who was tall, incredibly handsome and darkly dangerous.

Aching with hot, shameful feelings that had gotten her into trouble with Barnardo in New Orleans, she stalked over to her window and glanced out at the dark courtyard again. Standing there, wondering if anybody was there, she took another long sip.

Imagining a new, dangerous, dream lover in one of the windows, her skin warmed and her heart pounded.

Then, shocked at herself, she shook her head to clear her thoughts. She had to get to work. Turning away, she peeled off her gray jacket and slung it onto the newspapers she'd scattered under her easel. She gave no thought to how provocative her form-fitting sweater and her black miniskirt might appear without the jacket. After all, she was alone.

She moved about, her necklaces, bracelets and earrings catching the light and jingling. Josie kicked off her black leather mules and pranced around her huge canvas. Strutting about in her stockings on slippery newspapers, she drained the last of her wine and then set her glass beside her laptop. She placed her hands on her hips and leaned over the canvas, accentuating the twin curves of her bottom, which was thrust toward her window. Focused on the livid, purple beak of a painted gargoyle, she leaned over and put a lot of shapely leg on display, too.

She had a headache from her long day working at Brianna's gallery, so she rubbed her temples. A red, curling tendril came loose and fell against her cheek.

Even though Josie had almost no experience running a gallery, and her Cajun French left a great deal to be desired, Brianna had sworn Josie could cover for her while she and Jacques honeymooned.

"The gallery, plus my painting…trying to speak French… I don't think so, Brianna. You know how driven you are, compared to me."

Her skin the color of light brown sugar, Brianna was as tall and thin as a supermodel. She had huge dark eyes and straight black hair. Not that Bree had ever relied on her looks to get her where she wanted—except maybe when it came to snagging Jacques, a super-rich art broker she'd met at an art fair in London.

Josie had turned Bree down cold.

But that had been before Barnardo's exhibit had opened in a prominent New Orleans museum, starring Josie in the nude.

Suddenly the air in the little cubicle of Brianna's apartment felt bleak and stale and too heavy with the scent of her oils and Josie's own dying dreams.

Focus on today. On tonight. Not past or present failures.

She whirled on her canvas. Bits of stone bird and gigantic teeth seemed to be scattered all over the place. The brilliant colors that had fit so right last night confused her suddenly.

Thinking that fresh air and a glimpse of the Eiffel Tower might inspire her, Josie left the painting and went to the tall living-room window.

Without looking down at the snow-slicked cobblestones or across at the dark courtyard windows, she slid her window up. Then she leaned out, arching her long, slender neck, searching for the tower through the bare branches of the one-hundred-year-old trees.

Nothing.

Determined, she plopped down on the windowsill and eased her bottom farther out onto the icy ledge. Digging her heels under the radiator and gripping the wall with a hand, she leaned out some more.

Snowflakes landed on her cheeks and melted. Teeth chattering, butt freezing, snow dribbling down her face like teardrops, she smiled up at the iron lady glimmering above the roofline.

"Just like a gigantic Christmas ornament in a snow globe."

Forgetting the chill and her exhaustion and her suicidal, gravity-defying perch, she was in the process of leaning out even farther when a man whistled at her.

"Oh, my God! *You're real!*" Josie screamed.

Whirling wildly, she lost her grip on the wall.

For a dizzying instant a man's darkly handsome angular face spun crazily. Then she was falling toward bricks and cobblestones.

Grabbing for the wall, she latched on to the copper drainpipe that snaked up the building instead, and clung.

Her heart thundered. Instead of scooting back inside, she stayed in the window, never considering how the glow of the lamp behind her might silhouette her breasts, her narrow waist and her derriere.

Searching the windows for him, her temples began to pound. She felt a hairpin stabbing her scalp. Reaching up, she unpinned her hair. Then she shook her head, so that her red curls spilled in a shimmering mass over her shoulders.

Looking up, her gaze sought the long, black window opposite hers again.

The shade was up. For a second she was almost sure she saw a tall man moving about in the shadows.

A rush of heat coursed through her veins.

"Hello?" Holding her breath, she leaned out farther. "Is anybody there?"

Just the thought of him and the skin on her throat and shoulders prickled hotly. Her nipples grew tight and hard.

Was a stranger really watching?

Her blood beat faster. Blushing, she backed inside the window.

The strange feeling that a man really was watching her persisted. Waves of heat sizzled through her.

She should move away from the window. Instead her heartbeat sped up as she gazed across the courtyard. Hugging herself, imagining a dream lover, she forgot not to smile.

As she envisioned a man in the window, who had height and strength, who was somehow essential, a man who was enjoying this as much as she, her mind began to weave a fantasy.

Was he there? Her skin began to glow until soon she felt as hot as molten flame. Her heart raced.

A fierce, wild hunger swept her, for what, she did not know.

Two

Adam Ryder hadn't intended to be a voyeur, but when Miss Navarre's light snapped on across the courtyard, he instinctively moved closer to his own tall window. Then, like a hunter after prey, he waited in the dark.

Maybe if the overly warm room hadn't smelled moldy when he'd first walked in, he wouldn't have raised the shade or opened his window. None of that mattered now.

The instant he saw Josie Navarre take that tumble across her threshold and then start nibbling blueberries, one by one, the eroticism in her every gesture had made him burn.

Not that his taste ran to voluptuous redheads with masses of untamed curls. No, he preferred Abigail's rich black hair that was shorn in a short cap, and her exquisitely trim body that cut through any room she entered with such feminine class and precision that all male eyes turned to admire her…and *him*.

Nor did his taste run to the kind of exhibitionist who would pose nude for some enfant terrible of the art world, no matter how famous the bastard was. But was she an exhibitionist? Had she cooperated fully in the making of the raw, edgy video portrait of her taking a shower that had embarrassed her wealthy family?

Adam's mother had assumed the unscrupulous, paparazzi-seeking Barnardo had been her lover, that a woman like her would not discriminate. He thought once more of Abigail Morgan. She was the kind of wife any man would be proud to call his own.

Adam didn't travel well, and France was overrated in his opinion. The disdainful waiters were negligent; the taxi drivers hellishly rude—insane, really.

He did like his plump landlady, however, even though she'd tried to shortchange him. An inveterate gossip, she'd been more than willing to tell all about Mademoiselle Navarre.

"*La petite* keeps to herself. One man. Lucas. Not a boy-friend. Friend, think, poor little thing. She paints. She works. She brings me little presents her students make."

He'd been digging for dirt, not empathy. Still, it was good that the landlady thought the romance was in the beginning stages.

Because of the holiday crush and an ice storm in Austin, his plane had been ten hours late. Instead of being ready to tackle Miss Navarre, he was dead on his feet with jet lag.

If he'd gotten here this morning as scheduled, he would have marched straight into Ms. Navarre's gallery and written her a check to bow out of Lucas's life.

If only that were the case, the Ryders would be happily rid of Miss Navarre, and he wouldn't be spying on the delectable Miss Navarre as she pranced about her messy apartment nibbling blueberries and sipping red wine.

What the hell was she painting? Dissected body parts?

Too bad the untalented of the world rarely recognized their meager gifts for what they were—worthy of a hobby maybe, but not a career. And yet the violence and the mess of all those colors made him think of sex.

Wild, uninhibited sex with her.

Lust hit him hard and low and made his skin burn. With immense effort, Adam forced himself to think about his brother.

Lucas had come home raving about Paris, Hemingway, his novel and his plans to marry a Miss Josephine Navarre, who was obsessed with gargoyles.

"That's wonderful, dear," Marion, their mother, had said too sweetly. She rarely revealed her true concerns to anyone except Adam. "What's *she* like, dear?"

"She's an artist from New Orleans, living in Paris because her house on the bayou was flooded."

No mention of Barnardo.

"All her paintings were ruined. She was abandoned at birth by her mother, too."

Lucas had always had a soft spot for strays.

"What sort of artist?" Adam had demanded.

"Contemporary."

Adam had cut to the chase. "Is she making a living at it?"

"She's managing a gallery for a friend and teaching."

"Who are her people?"

"They're upper-class Creoles. At least her brothers and her mother are. Nobody knows who her biological father was."

"So, she's a bastard, dear?" Marion had whispered in that dangerous, saccharine tone of hers.

"From what I hear her stepfather was the bastard. Dominating. Impossible to please. Like our old man."

Marion's lips had thinned, and she'd gotten that haunted, defensive look only Adam understood. Lucas, who was rather imperceptive for a writer, had no inkling of his mother's feelings.

"When her mother's husband died, her mother told her sons that she'd lied about their baby sister dying at birth, that the little girl, Josie, had been entrusted to a devoted nurse, who'd then disappeared. The mother had hired a private detective who'd found Josie living in a swamp with illiterate trappers, the nurse's brother's family apparently. Before the nurse had died, she'd tried to contact Josie's mother but had reached her husband instead who'd insisted the child be left in the trappers' care. Josie's mother sent her sons to get her daughter. Josie was so filthy and wild, they weren't sure they'd ever tame her."

A little investigation into Miss Navarre's background was all it had taken to convince Marion Ryder, who adored and shamelessly spoiled and "protected" dear Lucas, that Josie was all wrong for her son.

The next day Marion had caught Adam alone.

"A low-class, Cajun swamp girl? A life-size video portrait of her naked in a public installation at the modern art museum? Can you imagine? Everyone in New Orleans has seen her without a stitch on!" Marion's eyes had widened in horror. "At least Celia's never sunk *that* low."

"Maybe we should wait to hear Miss Navarre's side of the tale."

"Always the lawyer! Don't you dare defend her! Do something!"

"I've got a lot going on. It's Christmas. Why don't you talk to Lucas?"

"Lucas?" She laughed. "You know how he is. Go to Paris now! Stop her!"

"With Abigail coming? This *is* my first vacation in a year!"

"I can't forget your marriage to Celia. Do you want that for Lucas? Or for the girl?"

Adam had gone cold.

Across the courtyard, the redhead was gazing out at the night and looking wistful. He forgot his mission and his mother. Heart pounding, Adam stared at her pale face and enormous eyes, at her half-opened mouth, and at her breasts. The rhythm of his heart sped up, and he forgot himself, forgot his brother, mother…everything.

The apartment suddenly felt so hellishly hot, he swiped his hand across his perspiring brow.

He expelled a harsh breath. Damn. Suddenly the bulge under his fly felt huge. Suddenly he wanted her enough to risk everything, even his brother's hatred, to have her.

Cursing, he willed himself to close his eyes, to shut her out, to slam out of his apartment and leave Paris.

Instead, he took an involuntary step toward the window.

Lucas. He was here to protect Lucas from making the same mistake he'd made.

Adam begrudged the effort it took to turn his thoughts back to Lucas.

Writing? Lucas fantasizing he was Hemingway.

Give me a break!

Writing was an excuse so Lucas could pretend he was doing something other than living off his trust fund. His free lifestyle, and the way he always bragged that he was a Ryder, had attracted a slew of undesirable "friends."

On the surface, Josephine Navarre hadn't sounded quite as bad as the rest. True, she had a chaotic history. Yes, she'd recently fallen for a notorious, narcissistic bad boy of the art world. Somehow the older, opportunistic Barnardo had shot a video of her when she was sitting nude in a white-tiled shower. Water had been streaming over her while she wept inconsolably, looking lost and young and incredibly vulnerable. Had she known she was being filmed?

Barnardo had cleverly crosscut these shots with clips of her wealthy family and their Middle-eastern friends and their offshore drilling rigs. He'd inserted footage of their gorgeous mansion in the Garden District along with images of ruined, lower-class, New Orleans neighborhoods. Then he'd shown their family-owned barges and crew boats in the Atchafalaya Swamp beside cypress trees that had been cut down and scattered like matchsticks.

Worst of all, Barnardo had exhibited his little reality montage in a leading museum during a recent oil crisis to much acclaim from environmentalist groups. The exhibit had garnered an excessive amount of publicity. Her family's empire had suffered a major financial hit and her brothers had been accused of corruption.

The Navarres had had the film seized, sued everyone involved and had packed Josie off to Paris.

Hell.

Even before his mother had convinced him to come, Adam had been concerned when Lucas had shown him a three-carat diamond ring and had told him he intended to propose to Miss Navarre on top of the Eiffel Tower.

Why? Because she was crazy about that particular edifice.

"You just said she won't even date you!"

"I'm in love, and so is she. There's this weirdo, who betrayed her, and this totally weirdo vow she made to herself—not to date anybody new for six months."

"The last thing you need is a wife. You haven't even established a career."

"Hell, who are you to talk to me? You were younger than me when you married Celia! Look what you did to her!"

"Exactly!"

So, here Adam was, alone in Paris, wasting his precious Christmas holidays spying on a pretty swamp girl who might or might not be as bad as his mother feared. Bottom line: he should be at the ranch courting Abigail.

Deliberately he lowered his gaze to Josie's breasts and thighs, meaning to make a sexual object of her again. Instead, his gaze focused on her long neck, which was soft and golden and lovely.

Now that was a bona fide work of art. He could see why that guy, Barnardo, might have been tempted to capture her on video.

Adam found himself wondering just how warm and soft she'd feel.

Something fierce and visceral possessed him. He swore again, silently, viciously.

He forgot Lucas. He wanted her for himself.

Her long lashes fluttered like fans against her cheeks and then stilled. With her eyes closed, she looked younger, vulnerable. Easily, Adam imagined a beautiful, dirtily clad, abandoned little girl, alone on a barge in a swamp, growing up with crude, uncaring people.

Suddenly he felt the baffling darkness without end she must have felt.

Why had she been crying in that video? Why had she told Lucas she'd been betrayed?

For a long moment she stood there. As if she sensed him, her breath clouded the pane. Her gaze filled with so much longing, he drew a sharp, painful breath and fought for control.

Fleetingly, forbidden memories of his brother Ethan, and

then Celia, swamped him, filling him with self-loathing. He shoved his hands into his pockets and strode away from the window. From *her*.

Why did this girl, whom he didn't even know, make him think of them? He began to pace back and forth like a caged animal.

Since those long-ago, fatally linked tragedies, Adam had controlled his memories, his ambition and his heart. Sexual desire was dangerous. He told himself that because he had such control, his life was a success.

Now, suddenly, because of Miss Navarre's stricken expression and sexy body, he felt a stranger to himself.

He'd come here to rid the family of her. Why then did he suddenly feel that the bedrock upon which his boots had been firmly planted for years was shifting? Why did looking at her make him feel that he was caught by a force as cataclysmic as an earthquake?

How could he save Lucas, when he couldn't even save himself?

He was tired. He should shut the shade and go to bed. Tomorrow was soon enough to deal with her.

Hardly realizing what he was doing, he snagged the little armchair at the desk and pushed it up to his window. His eyes never left her as he slowly sank down onto its plump cushion.

Her green eyes were wild and lost. She said something in French, which he didn't understand. Then with a smile, she switched to English.

"Watch me," she whispered as she leaned even farther out the window.

Suddenly her eyes lost their bravado.

He remembered Madame Picard's sad expression when she'd said, "Keeps to herself. One man. Lucas. Not a…"

Somewhere a siren blared. Then a cloud covered the moon.

She ran a hand through her hair and then down her sides.

Did she moan aloud? Or did he only imagine the husky sound?

She ran her hands lower, lower. At the last moment before she touched herself, she stopped, as if she realized what she was doing. *With a stranger.*

Her eyes widened. He told himself to look away, but something low and base and mysterious held them both in thrall.

He couldn't move or even breathe until she finally gasped and flew from the window and turned out her light.

He sucked in a choppy breath. And then another.

Suddenly he knew what he had to do.

And it wouldn't wait until tomorrow.

Three

She'd almost been tempted to touch herself.

Almost.

Josie's heels clattered on the stone steps as she ran recklessly down them. She shouldn't leave the apartment. She knew that, but something in the stranger's eyes had felt familiar and had made her feel compellingly connected to him on some deep, inexplicable level. At the same time, she'd felt larger and grander than her usual self, aware of exciting new possibilities. And yet lower, truer, too. Sex wasn't all sweetness and light. With her it could be a dark, all-consuming force.

Breathless, terrified in the cold darkness, scared of herself, of the handsome stranger who'd evoked such powerful responses, she stopped to catch her breath at the bottom of the stairwell.

Her eyes darted everywhere until he whistled, the same wolf

whistle as before, piercing her and the biting cold like a knife that burned straight to her heart.

Very tall, broad-shouldered, too, and dressed totally in black, the rugged stranger from the window leaned against the wrought-iron gate as if he owned it, as if he owned *her,* his big, powerful body blocking the only exit to the street.

He seemed feral and dangerous.

Watch me. Her words hummed in the icy haze between them.

The intensity of his heavily lidded, long-lashed dark eyes swallowed her, burned her, stripped her even. Only now, she felt shier than she had in her apartment when the gap of the courtyard had protected her.

She stared down at the innocent, white snow, afraid to meet his too-knowing, too-dangerous eyes.

With every second that passed, he seemed to grow taller and become more masculine, more threatening. Her heart sped up. She could feel her warm, naked skin under her clothing.

Suddenly the lifelong emptiness inside her made her feel too raw and needy. Thinking to escape him and the hungers he evoked, she gave a cry and began to back toward the stairs she'd just descended.

When he simply stood there and she realized he would not chase her, she felt safer. Her footsteps stilled on the cobblestones.

He whistled softly, admiringly. She clutched her jacket, shivering now, her breaths spurting like little puffs of smoke from her lips and nose into the still, cold air.

"I don't want to disappoint you, but…I—I'm not…that girl in the window…that bold girl."

He stopped whistling and stood perfectly motionless, his insolent gaze drifting up and down her body carelessly, as if she were already his property.

"What if you are? What if you don't know quite who you really are?"

"I'm not! I do!"

Part of her regretted that she'd displayed herself so lavishly and recklessly. But another part of her relished it. He was right, and she so hated that. Then her nose began to run from the cold, and she had to dab at it with her hand.

"Have it your way. The last thing I want is to argue," he drawled in that deep, possessive tone that made her shiver more violently as she imagined what such a man might want from her.

"So, you're American," she said.

He neither denied nor confirmed this.

"And I'm from Louisiana. New Orleans. Katrina…and all that." She shut up, afraid suddenly to tell him more.

His silent eyes regarded her as they had when she'd displayed herself in her window. His hot, male interest made her feel wild enough to risk anything.

"You're an artist."

"A painter," she corrected rather primly.

"Ah, yes. That canvas with all the red and purple. What exactly are you painting?"

"Gargoyles."

"Fearsome creatures," he said in what she assumed to be a mocking tone.

"They're very popular here in Paris," she said, feeling defensive. "There's even a tour of them. Maybe because I'm from New Orleans, I have a taste for the macabre."

"Really?" He didn't look all that interested in gargoyles as a topic of conversation.

"I shouldn't be here. It was rather reckless of me to come down."

"'Watch me,' I believe you said." His taunt was huskily soft. "I very much enjoyed your little show."

Heat crawled up her cheeks. She could think of no way to defend herself. "I should be upstairs painting. With my shade down!"

"Recklessness. Would anything ever get accomplished if it weren't for recklessness?"

"I regret what I did…and coming down."

"Do you?" He cocked his dark eyebrows as if he didn't quite believe her.

"I do. I swear it."

"Because I could be a serial killer?"

"Or worse."

"Isn't that part of the thrill? The unknown? Since we're all such pretenders in daily life, we get into ruts that can become exceedingly dull."

"Are you saying we all have secret agendas?"

"The most interesting people do. We know nothing about ourselves until a stranger in a window…" He paused.

"Reveals our truest nature," she finished, amazed that their minds seemed to be on such an identical track.

"The name's Adam. And just for the record, I'm much too dull and civilized to attack you."

"Josie," she whispered, not at all sure he was totally tamed. Deliberately she left off her last name—as he had.

"I'm a lawyer. I put real estate deals together. In Austin."

"Texas?" Like Lucas, she thought.

He nodded. "No hidden meanings in my career. There's only one agenda—greed, profit…the bigger the better."

"Adam. Nice name."

He thrust his hands in his pockets. "I shouldn't have watched you. I apologize. It was wrong of me." His mouth twisted. "Very wrong."

"Girlfriend back home?" she asked. "You were alone… missing her maybe. You saw me…."

His dark brows shot together as he moved across the darkness toward her. "I have a girlfriend," he admitted.

She saw that he was not dressed totally in black after all. His leather jacket was smooth, glossy black, and his boots were black, as well. But his overly long, denim jeans were actually a deep shade of navy.

"Long term relationship?"

"We're supposed to get married," he said.

So, why didn't he look happy about it?

"When?"

"No set date."

"Why not?"

"You ask too many questions."

"It's called getting acquainted. It's called making sure you're not that serial killer. So, why no set date?"

"Can we leave her the hell out of this?" His voice was bleak, angry suddenly, more at himself than at her, she thought.

She liked that he seemed to have a conscience, but she was suddenly too curious to stop. "So, *were* you missing her? Is that why you watched me?"

His eyes grew hot and dark, and she felt herself blushing again.

"I shouldn't have watched you," he repeated.

"So you're the Boy Scout type?"

"Eagle Scout. But that was a lifetime ago."

"So, now that we've apologized, maybe I should go back upstairs. You can call your girlfriend, and I can paint."

"What about you? Boyfriend?"

She thought of dear, sweet Lucas and his eager, little-boy message on Brianna's machine earlier in the evening.

"Maybe there's the possibility of one…in the near future. But I was burned recently. I'm not sure I'm ready yet."

Adam's eyes narrowed. Something about the shape of his broad shoulders and square head reminded her of someone.

She cocked her head, studying him with new interest. "Have we met before?"

He shook his head. "If we had, you'd remember." His voice and eyes were cocky.

"You're pretty sure of yourself."

"You'd remember." His gaze locked on her face as it had when he'd stared at her from his apartment, now seeming to land on the moist heat of her lips.

A car rushed past her building, slinging slush, its headlights illuminating the bare branches above them. She focused on the sudden clenching of his jaw, on his high cheekbones that stood out like blades. He had a long straight nose and arrogant chin. There was a slight scar above his right eye.

He was handsome. Too handsome. Rugged but well-educated and polished, too.

She didn't do well with handsome and polished. She fell too hard, gave too much, and the handsome, polished guys always walked when they discovered her real roots.

The black sky was clearing. Suddenly there were stars every-where, shooting, soaring stars that made her feel alive.

He looked up, following her gaze, and then back at her, suddenly on full alert again.

"I know it's late for a Texan, but there's a bistro at the end of the block. The owner told me he'd stay open Christmas Eve," she said, swooping around him and heading toward the gate he'd barred earlier. "He's a wonderful chef and he has a fabulous wine cellar. I'm something of a *pilier* here."

"Pilier?" He copied her accent so exactly she was almost jealous. Obviously, he had a talent for languages.

"A *pilier* is a regular," she explained and smiled.

Laughing, he repeated the word. "My French leaves a lot to be desired."

"Mine does, too. You see, I…" She stopped. The last thing she wanted to tell him about was anything having to do with her childhood.

The cold was seeping through the soles of her thin shoes, and her toes were going numb. She shivered. "I'm getting cold."

"Would you like for me to buy you a cup of coffee at your bistro?" he asked. "Or I have a coffeemaker in my apartment. And my apartment's closer."

"I don't think so," she whispered shyly, shrinking from the too-heated awareness in his eyes, only to stumble backward.

Ice crunched behind her. Swiftly his large, warm hand closed over her elbow, sending a high-voltage jolt through her jacket and sweater as he steadied her.

"You'll just love the bistro," she whispered as she jumped free of him.

Then she ran out onto the narrow street onto the main thoroughfare lined with imposing mansions that had mansard roofs. Above these tall, shadowy buildings, the curves of her favorite historic domes rose against the black sky. Not that he seemed to notice the marvelous architecture as he loped to catch her.

"Not so fast," he warned. "There's ice."

"Yes, but isn't it beautiful?"

He made no comment on the tracery of white Christmas lights in the trees or on the sparkling snow. When she hurried past a pharmacy, a closed pastry shop, several unlit bistros and bars, he caught up. Matching his long strides to hers, he cast curious glances inside each establishment.

Soon she wished she wasn't so acutely conscious of his tall, powerful body beside hers.

"Walk slower," he ordered.

Afraid he might touch her again, she obeyed.

Desperately she fought to act cool and nonchalant, but every time they passed under a streetlight or the moon came out from behind a cloud, she glanced up at him and experienced a baffling, unnerving sense of familiarity.

"You definitely remind me of someone," she said.

"We've never met," he repeated.

Then why did he look alarmed before he turned away?

She'd had a long day and a glass of wine. It was Christmas Eve, which brought back all the old issues of other Christmas Eves when she'd been lonely and alone after sadly, her guardian had died.

Whatever was eluding her about him refused to surface.

But it would; probably at the worst possible moment.

Four

Adam's grip tightened on his knife and fork when their tall, snooty waiter stared down his nose at him. Without a word the man flung a basket of rye bread with superthick crusts, thick slabs of butter and a platter of escargots—large snails Josie had explained—down onto the middle of their table.

She ordered everything in rapid, fluent-sounding French while the waiter rudely rolled his eyes and made awful faces, which caused her to blush.

When Adam frowned at the man, he hurried away.

"French waiters," Adam muttered. "Do I bring out the worst in them or what?"

"It's probably me, my French, but I'm sure we shouldn't take his behavior personally. It's a French waiter thing."

"Glad you're philosophical."

"Moving on. I don't usually entice men at windows," she blurted.

"Does that mean I'm special?"

"No!"

"Hidden agendas," he teased. "Yours...and mine. You're here and so am I. You left your apartment. You asked me out."

"My feet were cold."

"Still, I'm flattered...by all your attentions this evening."

She blushed again, and so charmingly Adam felt her heat all the way across the small round table. Suddenly he was glad of the block of wood between them that kept her a safe distance away.

What was it about her? Why did he want her?

She was not *that* beautiful.

He eyed her slim, golden throat, her breasts. He wanted to touch her too much, to pull her close, to nuzzle her beautiful neck and drink in the smell of her skin. He wanted to lick her, to taste her, to devour her.

"I'm not usually a damned voyeur, either," he muttered fiercely.

"Obviously, we bring out the worst in each other."

She ran her fingernails along the top of her wineglass and looked away. Then with a frown, she tore off a hunk of dark bread and began to spoon the escargot onto the little plate in front of her.

"So, why did you come out with me?" he asked.

"We couldn't just keep standing there. Not when my toes were numb."

"I feel like kissing your toes."

She looked away, and he knew why. Because to look at each other was to drown, to surrender to something wild and dark and unnamable.

Their eyes met again and not quite by accident. Again, he felt a zing of fiery warmth, and she quickly lowered her gaze.

Suddenly he was very glad she'd chosen this bistro with its smoke-smudged walls and tables filled with other people rather than his apartment, where they would be totally alone with a bed in the next room. Even here, it was all too easy to imagine her in his apartment, willingly naked in his arms, lying underneath him on that narrow bed, her soft body a perfect fit. She would be warm, silky, tight. She'd taste delicious. In his mind, he stripped her and got harder as he kept imagining her naked underneath him, writhing.

He clenched his fists. He had reasons to fear her. Memories…

Flickering candlelight glimmered in her red curls. Her green eyes sparked with childlike delight every time she looked up shyly from slathering globs of butter on her thick rye crust.

She was eating the crusts, his favorite part of the loaf. Oddly, he liked that they had that in common.

"Do you want some bread?" she whispered.

"Not yet."

"It will be all gone."

"I'll order more."

She lowered her gaze, and he tried to concentrate on the odors of wine and the bubbling sauces, on the smell of scallions, mushrooms and garlic. He should direct the conversation to Lucas and then proceed from there with directness and boldness and honesty.

"So, tell me about yourself. Who are you? Why are you in Paris?" she asked as she began gobbling a buttery snail drenched in parsley sauce with excessive relish.

Now! Tell her you're Lucas's brother!

"Ladies first," he hedged.

She stabbed a snail and held it up to his lips, her gaze lingering too long on his mouth.

Undone, he shook his head. He had to get this little interview the hell over with.

"They're quite good," she said before plopping the greasy little sucker into her mouth. Swallowing, she sipped her jewel-red cabernet and stabbed another snail with her tiny fork. He watched as she swirled it in the thick parsley sauce.

She ate another snail and then smiled. "Delicious! I'm so tired of eating alone, of doing everything alone."

He remembered Madame Picard calling her a poor little thing.

"That's a trouble with foreign countries," he said.

"Yes, if you aren't totally fluent in the native language, it's hard to talk to people."

"When we ordered, you sounded pretty damn fluent."

"*Oui.* My accent is terrible, though. Cajun French. I—I didn't study real French…until high school. I'm afraid to open my mouth here because of how vulgar I sound. I sort of live life on the surface. I've been here nearly a month."

"Long enough to become very lonely and feel alienated?"

"Yes." Her brilliant eyes flared with gratitude that he understood.

"Loneliness. So that's why you came down tonight?"

"I guess."

"I know what that's like," he said. "Even back home in Texas surrounded by all my associates, ranch hands, clients and family, I feel lonely."

"Even with your girlfriend?"

He refused to think about Abigail. Instead he thought of his huge modern house, constructed of glass and steel, on its limestone hill. How cold and lifeless it always seemed…even with Bob there to run things so perfectly.

"I dread going home at night," he said. "My house is beautiful with towering glass windows. The whole city of Austin looks like jewels scattered beneath it."

"Big houses are the loneliest houses," she said.

"Maybe that's why I work all the time," he said.

"Do you have friends?"

"Yes, but my friendships are all about networking and getting ahead."

That was how Abigail operated, too. She was brilliant, super-efficient. People had to be worth knowing careerwise or socially for her to bother with them.

"But that sounds so cold," Josie said.

"Maybe. Outside of work, I rarely talk to these people."

Strange, that he hadn't realized how lonely he was before tonight…. With Josie.

For no reason at all he remembered how easy he used to feel with both his brothers before Ethan's death. Back then, Adam had had real friendships and real feelings.

With a quick frown Adam killed that dangerous train of thought by changing the subject. "How about you?" he said.

He asked Josie about her life. When she began to open up about herself, about her brothers, about her awful childhood in the Atchafalaya Swamp, Adam began to relax as he hadn't in years.

"So, for years I thought I was swamp trash, and then these tall young men roared up to our barge in an airboat. It was like a dream."

She smiled. "They totally intimidated me. Even before they told me who I was and brought me home. Home being this enormous, southern mansion in one of the oldest, most prestigious neighborhoods in New Orleans. I spoke this terrible, back-water French none of them understood. And my manners were wild. I didn't know how to hold a fork or a knife. I was dirty, shoeless and in ragged jeans. The soles of my feet were so black and tough, it took six months of scrubbing and wearing shoes all the time to turn them pink and soft."

She sighed. "My mother stared at me with such horror that day on her veranda. She couldn't believe what had happened to me. I'd dreamed of having a mother like her, and my brothers told me that the minute their father died she'd begun to weep for the daughter she'd been forced to give away. So, she wanted me, I guess. But that day I didn't know that. All I saw was how she frowned. When she ordered the maid and her daughter, Brianna, to bathe me in a big sink in the utility room adjoining the kitchen. Even after they finished, she didn't act happy about my coming into the main house. She told me not to touch anything. I got so scared I ran, and so I broke one of her favorite china figurines. We both cried for hours."

Josie paled at the memory.

"I liked going away to college better." Her smile brightened. "I got to study art. Not that it was easy to find my medium or my muse."

Although he listened, he couldn't really figure out what a muse was exactly. She even mentioned Barnardo in passing, frowning as she said she wasn't free to give out details because of pending litigation.

She really did seem to be a nice person. He felt like a heel for coming here to buy her off. But not for watching her. That bizarre lapse held some elusive truth he couldn't evade.

She told him all about Brianna, her boss, who was the daughter of her mother's onetime maid.

"Brianna was the only person I ever really felt close to as a teenager in that grand house."

He stared at her, wishing heartily that she wasn't such a nice person.

"But, Adam, you haven't told me much about yourself," she murmured. "Most men…that's all they talk about."

He shifted uneasily, dropping his napkin. He leaned down and picked it up. "I already know about me."

"But I don't. If you won't talk to me, I'll think you have something to hide. Why, you haven't even told me your last name. I know you're from Austin and you're a lawyer and that you have a big house. But that's all."

She leaned toward him with a slippery mollusk dripping off her fork again. "Last one. You really should try it…."

He was about to shake his head again, but her big eyes were bright with delight. "Oh, hell, why not live dangerously?"

"Exactly," she whispered.

He opened his mouth, and she poked the slithery thing inside.

"It really is surprisingly delicious," he said after two chomps.

"I told you." She smiled, her eyes as alight as a thrilled child's.

He was about to swallow when she asked, "So, what brings you to Paris over the holidays?"

"Actually…it's because of my brother…. L—"

When he gulped, the damn snail jumped into his windpipe and got stuck. He tried to swallow but managed only a hoarse, wheezing sound, and the thing stuck tighter.

Whoever heard of anybody choking on something as slippery as a damned snail?

Strangling, his throat tightened convulsively as he fought to swallow. Grabbing the edges of the table, he stood up.

"Adam!" she shrieked, maybe because his eyes were bulging. Then she screamed for a waiter. "Garçon!"

None of the snooty bastards came.

He coughed, choking, wheezing.

"Adam! Oh, my God! Hang on!"

She rushed around the table, got behind him and pounded her fists between his shoulder blades. When he staggered, she circled him with her arms. Then she jabbed her fists in the center of his chest, right above his sternum.

"Adam! You're going to be okay! Just hold on while I…"

She jabbed upward. The room, with its gray walls and copper pans, blackened. Clawing, choking, he crashed forward.

The next thing he knew, his cheek was on the cold, wooden floor. He wasn't fighting to breathe anymore. All he could manage were hoarse, whistling sounds.

Vaguely he was aware of her screaming, of the pandemonium of other people shouting and racing around, too. Glass shattered somewhere.

He was almost unconscious when strong arms lifted him and a huge fist rammed into his gut so hard the snail popped out.

Somebody hit him again. He felt a mouth on his. Not hers. A couple of forced breaths down his ravaged throat. Then he opened his eyes and gulped in air on his own.

He looked up. A dozen red-faced, scowling waiters in long aprons towered over him, all yelling incomprehensible French at him and her. Josie was kneeling beside him, ignoring the waiters now and stroking his cheek with the back of her hand. Never had anything felt so soft or so tender as her fingertips grazing his skin.

Slowly her beautiful face came into focus, her luminous, densely fringed green eyes seeming to see all the way to his soul.

When her hand closed over his, he held on as if his life depended on it.

When the fuss died down and he was on his feet and himself

again, he went to the men's room and washed his face and hands. When he returned, he ordered their dinners and a fresh loaf of bread to be packed in boxes. When all was done to his satisfaction, he paid the bill.

"Do you mind finishing our meal in my apartment?" he murmured in her ear, his voice still hoarse and scratchy from the snail. "I made such a spectacle of myself, I don't feel like staying with everybody watching." Hell, not when he felt like a wimp.

"Of course," she said as if she were aware of everyone's fascination with them, too. She pointed out two iced, sugar cookies on a shelf and said she wanted them for dessert.

"I so should resist them," she said.

"Not tonight, you shouldn't. You should have whatever you want."

He carried their take-home boxes out the door. When they stepped into the icy dark, she slipped her arm through his, and they walked backed to their building, their hips touching from time to time.

"No more snails," she said when he'd spread their feast out onto the tiny wooden table in his tiny kitchen. "I could have killed you!"

"You were quick on your feet. Marvelous. Maybe you saved my life."

"I think you're overstating the case. That waiter…"

"Don't remind me of him."

He stared down at her beautiful, shining face and cupped her chin. "You were great. Incredible. I will never forget how you looked when I came to."

When she reached for the sack of cookies, he shook his head and moved them onto the stove.

She laughed. So did he. Then an embarrassed hush fell between them again.

Suddenly all he saw were her eyes and her lush, pink lips. All he heard were his own heartbeats.

When she glanced toward the cookies, he took her hand and pressed it tightly. A shock of awareness built inside him again.

Without thinking, he tugged her closer. When she began to tremble, a fatal sense of inevitability drummed in his blood.

Death and sex were very close—at least in the primitive male mind. At least in his. He remembered his wildness after Ethan…Celia…

"So, why did you come to Paris?" she said even as her satiny palm melted inside the heat of his own closed hand.

Suddenly he wanted desperately to pull her closer, to tell her all about himself. Suddenly he even wanted to tell her about Celia, about all his regrets…and failings. It seemed very important, all-important, for her to know him and be warned.

Oddly, the last thing he felt like discussing was Lucas and the business at hand.

So, he said, "I don't think it matters anymore…why I came. I saw you…and I know you a little, so now everything's changed."

"For me, too."

When his arms circled her, she moaned. Her hands slid around him, her fingers kneading the small of his back.

Frantic, she tugged his shirt out of his jeans. As soon as she found hot, naked skin, her hands roamed hungrily.

He lowered his mouth to hers, and after that first sweet taste of her, his tongue dipped inside her lips again and again. In the next instant her breathing was as labored as his, and she was sucking on his tongue.

"Adam…oh, Adam…."

Her hands found his fly, and when her burning fingertips

slipped beneath his waistband, his pulse quickened, if that were possible.

Then she found him, grabbed him, circled him, stroking the damp tip until he lost all control.

Strong, dark emotions chased through him. When the kissing and stroking went on and on, his fierce hunger built. Just when he would have carried her to the bedroom, her hand froze around his erection.

"What am I doing?" She loosened her fingers. "Oh, what am I doing?"

Eyes widening, she pushed him away.

He groaned.

"What must you think of me?" she said.

"I want you," he said. "And you want me."

For a long moment, her frightened gaze darted anywhere but to him. Then she ran to the window.

"I swear—I'm not like this usually," she said. "Not that I haven't had a slip…or two." Her expression darkened. "That's why I can't have another one."

"Don't apologize."

"I don't know what's come over me."

"It's called sex. It's a basic, primal need."

"I'm not an animal."

"I didn't mean it that way. I like you, or, at least, I like what I know of you. Look, why don't we forget what nearly happened and sit down and eat. Afterward, you can do whatever you decide. Go or stay."

She turned and stared at him and then at the food that he'd spread out on the table.

"I won't pounce. I swear." He clenched his hands into fists. Then he opened them wide and held them up.

She drew in a deep breath. Then she smiled. Ducking her head, she scooted past him back into her chair.

He handed her a napkin and sat down across from her.

The silence was awkward at first as he fought to get himself back under control. Then silverware began to clatter.

For the first time in his life he didn't have a clue about what to do next.

Five

One kiss, and I put my hands down his pants!

Josie was shaking as she set her fork down.

He pushed his plate to one side. "Full?"

"So full." When she sipped the last of her wine, he refilled her glass.

"I—I really should go. I never… I've never…"

"Look, things are happening pretty fast for me, too," he said.

His dark eyes were warm, kind. He seemed so agreeable, she forgot to be afraid.

"You know, you're really nice. I didn't think you would be so nice…. I mean, when I saw you…in the window. I imagined you to be much more dangerous."

"Disappointed?"

She shook her head. "I like it that you're not some weirdo or bad guy, who's out to get me even when I sort of test the limits."

His mouth thinned.

"You haven't done anything but behave like a Boy Scout."

He pushed back from the table. "Like I said, my Eagle Scout are in the past. Are you really done with your *oeufs brouillés* and black truffles?"

"Bien sûr." Sipping more wine, she relaxed a little. "I ate too much. I wasn't even hungry until I started eating those snails. Oops, I'm sorry. Promise! I won't mention them again."

He stabbed one of her truffles and ate it. "It's okay. But it's late, and you did say you wanted to go. It's beginning to seem like forever since I slept. Jet lag. It's hit me again. I'll walk you home."

Maybe it was the wine. Maybe she was simply perverse. But now that he'd backed off, suddenly strange new yearnings were shimmering inside her again. She wanted to touch his hand, to caress his long, tanned fingers, to entwine them around hers.

Maybe because he wanted her gone, she felt it safe to stay and tease him. Thus, she pointed to her little sack. "My cookies! We haven't had dessert!"

Smiling, he got up and handed them to her.

She opened the sack. "Thank you for forcing me to eat dinner first. I'm afraid I love sweets, too much, as you can probably tell...since I'm the last thing from skinny."

His dark, hot gaze skimmed her breasts. "You're lovely... just as you are."

Lovely. At his husky tone, her toes curled. With a sharp intake of breath, she ripped the sack open and bit the head off a snowman.

Gooey icing melted in her mouth. "I should have bought a dozen of these."

He gobbled his half whole while she sliced the other cookie in two. Then he smiled as he watched her savor every sweet, delicious bite.

"What are you thinking?" she whispered.

"That you're too sexy. That I should take you home before we get in to real trouble."

She wanted him to put his arm around her and pull her close. When he stood and merely brushed his lips against her brow before he backed away, she felt a bitter pang of disappointment.

He touched her waist. "I'll walk you home."

She picked up her wineglass and drained it. When he opened the door and hurried her down his staircase and then back up to her landing, they stood breathless in the dark at her door. She leaned against the cold, stone wall. As she dug for her key, she half hoped he would kiss her again.

But he waited in the icy dark until her keys jingled. Only then did his hand close over hers. Again, just that slight, unexpected contact was enough to make her sizzle. She jumped back and he inserted the long, heavy key into the lock and opened her door easily.

When she stepped across her threshold, he backed away.

"You could come in. I—I could show you my painting."

Shaking his head, he backed into the shadows.

She shut her door and pressed her cheek against the rough wood. Feeling lost, she listened for his retreating footsteps as she shook off her jacket and dropped it onto the floor.

Finally, she gave up and sank to the floor and curled up on the jacket. Her heart thudding, she waited for several more long minutes. When she still hadn't heard him leave, she got up and opened her door.

"Adam?"

Golden light splashed from behind her, so she couldn't see him watching her from the dark. But she could feel him.

"Adam?"

"You shouldn't have opened that damned door," he rasped.

"Why didn't you go?"

"Hell."

"Then you do want me…maybe a little?"

"Hell." He sounded wild and fierce.

Thrilled, she tiptoed across the frigid darkness and put her hand on his.

He jerked free but not before she'd felt his heat. "Go back inside, you little fool, before you freeze to death."

"Oh, I don't think I'll freeze." With every word, her boldness grew. "I said watch me. Now I say, kiss me."

When he gasped, she reached up and wound her fingers around his neck. Inhaling his clean, male scent as well as the tart, spicy fragrance of his aftershave, she brushed the thick hair off his collar.

Just that was enough to make him shudder violently.

Pressing her soft, curvy body against his solid, angular frame, she sprang onto her tiptoes. Licking her lips, she parted them before molding her body to his.

Instantly, his mouth hardened on hers and his tongue slid inside. His excitement excited her. She moaned, pressing herself to him even more tightly.

With a groan, he gathered her close. Wrapping his leather jacket around her, he shoved her against the icy wall and ate her mouth with his lips and tongue while his hips ground against her pelvis. Mashed between the stone wall and his big body, she hugged him tighter.

As suddenly as he'd begun, he stopped. "Go back inside."

"No."

She took his hands and turned their rough palms to her lips and blew warm kisses into them. Then she shaped those heated palms to her breasts. She cupped his face, exploring the bone structure of his marvelous cheekbones with the pads of her thumbs, before tracing the rough texture of his jawline with her soft fingertips.

On a fierce shudder, he buried his lips in the hollow of her throat, kissing the pulse that beat there. When he found her mouth again, he kissed her longer and harder. Finally, he lifted her and hauled her into the apartment. With a single kick, the door slammed shut behind him.

He pressed her up against the wall and yanked her skirt down and her sweater up. Within seconds his hands were undoing the fastenings of her bra and she was naked. Then his fingers were inside her, and she was wet and moaning at his expert touch, even as they sank together onto the soft folds of her jacket and skirt and sweater that were pooled beside her door.

He unzipped his pants and would have entered her, but she stopped him with a little, throat-clearing sound.

"C-condom!"

"Damn," he muttered. "Suitcase. Back in my apartment. I never intended for this to happen."

"Bathroom. Second shelf! To the left! Hurry!" She chewed her bottom lip, which was raw and burning from his kisses. "Oh, and I never intended this to happen, either. They're not mine," she added virtuously. "They're Brianna's. You see, I'm on a no-sex…er…no-man regime in Paris."

"Like hell you are."

"Something terrible happened to me the last time I…" She stopped.

"I won't hurt you." He kissed her hard on the mouth again.

When he didn't stop kissing her, she forced herself to come up for air. "Condom."

"Right."

In a flash he was off her. He stood, towering above her. She bit her lips until he came back.

When he sank to his knees and put the thing on and was about to lower himself toward her, she held up a hand.

"No! Two! Use two."

He laughed and then cursed as he struggled to comply with her request.

Then his hard arms came around her. Before she knew it, he shoved himself inside her. Erect, pulsing, he filled her, stretching her warm, secret, satiny flesh as no man ever had. Filled as well were all those empty, wounded places in her heart.

What was it about him? At last, maybe for the first time, she felt accepted for herself alone.

He pumped vigorously and her nails dug in to his shoulders.

"Harder. Faster," she urged.

"I've got to stop…or…"

"You promised not to stop, remember?"

He slammed into her, once, twice.

It was over too soon for both of them.

Afterward, he was wet and hot and gasping for each breath. She was perspiring heavily, and her nails were embedded in his shoulders. Tenderly he pulled her closer and touched his damp forehead against hers. Stroking her cheek with a fingertip, he kissed the tip of her nose.

He removed her hand and fingernails from his shoulders and cupped her chin. "Next time will be all for you. It's been a while. You felt too good. I couldn't stop."

She felt a secret thrill to have given him so much pleasure. Shivering, she said, "I didn't want you to stop. I loved being with you. I—I feel like I've known you forever."

Gently he lifted her to her feet. "Where's your bedroom?"

Without speaking, she took his hand and pulled him down the short hallway.

He ripped the thick, cross-stitched covers back and laid her down on Brianna's crisp, cool, embroidered sheets. Lying on her back, Josie looked up and saw the bare trees shimmering in the moonlight beyond his broad shoulders. The stars seemed wilder, she thought. Or was it her?

Leaning back, he ripped off his boots and sent them clunking against the wooden floor. He peeled off his black shirt, and then his dark jeans, flinging them after the boots.

When Adam leaned over her, spread her legs and lowered his head between them, she gasped in total awe when he found and licked the exact perfect spot without the slightest hesitation. He knew what he was about.

Probably she shouldn't let a man she'd just met do such an intimate thing, but with him, all barriers seemed to be down.

As his tongue drifted over damp, velvet, pulsing skin, her legs went limp and fell wider apart, offering her entire being to him.

Josie hummed, purred and grew even hotter as Adam stroked her to the point of rapture. But each time she nearly exploded, he stopped and left her shaking with desire. Each time she gripped his head and brought his mouth back, begging him to kiss her again. Then he'd begin again, only slower, so that when she finally exploded against his lips, his tongue was deep inside her.

For an endless time he continued to lick while her climax went on and on.

"Your turn," she finally whispered.

Still gasping and shaking from his carnal caresses, she crawled down the length of his muscular body. Her tangled curls skimming his skin, she took the moist, salty tip into her lips. He was so huge and male and deliciously salty, she moaned. Finally, she began moving her head back and forth, tasting him, reveling in his length as he bloomed to a bigger, hotter size inside her mouth.

She wanted to taste him so much, but he had immense control. Finally, he rolled away, pulled her up into his arms and plunged inside her, his fierce possession even hotter than before.

She went rigid, frantic. "Condom…"

He went still. "Damn. Sorry about that. Honey, I'm so sorry."

On a ragged shudder, he pulled out. Breathing from between clenched lips, he threw his head back. It took him a while before he regained enough control to get up and stalk the short distance down the cold hall to the bathroom.

She was terrified. Should she run to the shower?

He had the thing on when he came back. No way could she leave him now.

He climbed into bed, slid his arms around her and thrust inside her again. Each time he plunged, he felt bigger, harder, wilder.

Afterward, she clung, feeling his fierce, rippling tension cording every muscle. She wept, wanting this wild, wondrous man to ride her forever. Then suddenly, she soared, too, crying out his name again and again.

As before, he was sweet afterward, holding her close, stroking her hair, whispering love words and kissing away her tears. She felt vulnerable, open, adored and so safe in his arms, so protected, as if nothing could ever hurt her or make her doubt herself again.

"I was afraid…all the time…maybe all my life," she whispered. "Ever since I was a little girl, even after my brothers found me, I've always felt alone. Until tonight with you."

The muscles in his arms bunched. Then he sucked in a sharp breath. Wordlessly, he drew her even closer so that the soles of her feet lay on top his.

"What were you so afraid of?"

"In the Atchafalaya Swamp, where I grew up, there were always these awful sounds. I would hear birds or animals scream, and I knew that they were being eaten alive. There were awful things out there. White alligators, even."

"Well, you're in Paris, safe in my arms."

"Yes."

He held her, stroking her hair, kissing her brow, her closed eyelids, and then her throat with lips that felt incredibly erotic, maybe because his sex was still deeply embedded inside her.

"I feel so happy," she said.

"You have a beautiful neck," he said.

"Thank you. But I'm too fat everywhere else."

"You're perfect."

"I'm too fat."

"Does every woman in America feel that way? Is that a rule or something…to belong to some secret sisterhood?"

She laughed.

"You're perfect. So perfect. Sexy. And I'd be the one to know since I've now seen and tasted every glorious part of you. Not only are you beautiful, you're delicious, too."

She blushed, wanting to hear more, but he drew himself up and off her. She felt a sense of loss until he lowered his mouth to her wet secret again and began to lick and kiss her all over again. Again, his tongue probed so deeply and intimately inside her, he sent shock waves throughout her body.

When her skin was tingling everywhere, she spread her legs

and would have shuddered against his mouth, but he pulled away and made her wait.

"What are you doing?"

"Counting cows," he said.

She frowned. "How many cows?"

"I don't know. I'll tell you when I'm done counting."

Then he made her wait—five excruciatingly long minutes, the longest five minutes of her life.

When he began kissing her again, he kept at it until she clutched his neck and her body arced against his lips.

"Merry Christmas," he whispered as she collapsed onto the mattress.

She stroked his rough jaw with a trembling fingertip. "I can't believe I met you…that this happened. That you think I'm perfect. Tonight seems too good to be true."

"Could be," he muttered, his body tensing, his voice suddenly fierce and unbearably dark.

When sirens screamed outside, she shivered.

"I don't really know you," she said.

His arms tightened around her. "No." Once again his voice was low and hard.

Not wanting to feel so afraid, she squeezed her eyes shut and laid her head in the center of his chest and held on to him for dear life.

"Go to sleep." He kissed her brow gently, so gently, but strangely his tenderness and sweet kiss made her more afraid.

She didn't want to go to sleep because she didn't want to wake up and find him gone.

The next morning when her eyelids fluttered against the pale brightness filling the room, frost glimmered on the bare branches of the trees. The dank, heavy scent of the Seine felt thick in the bedroom. She sighed, blissfully aware of the warmth of Adam's heavy body lying beside hers.

She lay motionless, savoring his nearness. She'd slept well, without any of her nightmares. And he was still here.

For a long time she lay quietly, feeling content and totally happy. More than anything she wanted to hold on to this moment and to him forever.

But who was he? Before him she'd been disappointed in love so many times. Would she want him when she knew who he was?

Six

Josie knew the exact second Adam woke up. Not that he rolled over or yawned or said anything.

His breathing simply changed.

Silent seconds of awareness ticked by before he slowly turned and kissed her brow.

"I'm sure I look terrible," she whispered shyly.

"Beautiful." Gently his knuckles grazed her brow.

"Bed hair."

He smoothed her tangled curls.

"Ouch!"

"Sorry. I love your hair."

"It's always such a mess. Incorrigible. Wild."

"How about a shower?" he whispered, his dark eyes on fire.

"The apartment's too cold."

He sprang out of bed and heaped covers on top of her. "You don't happen to have a spare toothbrush?"

"Several. Bathroom. Same shelf where the…condoms…"

"Gotcha."

When he struck a match in the kitchen, she heard the whoosh of gas burners. He strode back down the hall and turned on the shower. When he returned to her bedroom, he wore a white towel around his waist and smelled of her soap and shampoo. Smiling, pulling her covers up around her neck, she sat up in bed to admire the sleek pull of tanned muscles when he turned his back and rustled in her closet for something to wear.

She shut her eyes and sucked in a breath. When the mattress dipped and he knelt over her again, he was wearing a black robe that must be Jacques's. Brianna's thick, black satin robe was slung over his arm.

He slid the covers back, wrapped her in Brianna's robe and helped her out of bed. She sighed with pleasure at the softness of the cool satin sliding against her skin. Hand in hand they scampered to the tiny bathroom, which was snug and warm after he closed the door. Quickly he peeled the robe off her shoulders. While her bare toes curled against the cold tile floor, he cupped her breasts and then ran his lips down her back. Starting at her neck, his tongue lingered over every vertebra while steam poured from the shower.

"Counting cows again?" she whispered as the wet warmth of his tongue against her skin made her breath catch.

"No. It's still early. You haven't driven me to that yet today."

In the shower, he scrubbed her with soap and let her soap him all over, too. When they were clean and slick and he was impressively aroused, he pushed her against the tile wall. Two thrusts and they both exploded.

Afterward she felt dazed and limp. He laughed when she clung, calling her Miss Spaghetti Legs. Then he soaped her all over again. When he helped her out of the shower, he grabbed a thick white fleecy towel and dried her.

"Do you have any food in your pantry?" he asked. "Eggs, maybe?"

"Ouefs?" she teased, feeling vaguely disappointed that their morning love session was over. Never had she felt so insatiable. "I have *ouefs* and bread."

"Then I'll leave you to the mirror while I scramble a few *ouefs* and maybe burn some toast or something."

"So you cook, too?"

"Don't get your hopes up." He kissed the tip of her nose and was gone.

In the bathroom she put on her makeup, or at least, the basics, which included lipstick and eye shadow. She ran a brush through her wild curls.

When she went to the bedroom and saw the tangled sheets and his jeans and shirt still on the floor, she began picking his things up. First, she folded his shirt and placed it on top of her dresser. When she picked up his jeans, a sleek, black leather wallet slid onto the floor, spilling six or seven credit cards.

She picked up the smooth, calfskin wallet. The swirling *R* engraved in the glossy leather drew her gaze, and she began to tremble without knowing why. Still shaking, she folded his jeans and laid them over the back of her chair. Then she placed his wallet and cards on top of his shirt on the dresser. When she grabbed his boots near the window, she saw identical swirling *R*s on each boot.

Feeling weak and sick, she lifted his wallet and held it next to those *R*s on Adam's tall, black boots.

An image of Lucas's tan leather glove emblazoned with that same swirling *R* flickered in the back of her mind.

Collapsing on the bed, she hissed in a long breath. Then with a cry, she threw the boots and wallet against the wall.

I told everybody about you, and they're all...happy... except...my older brother...but, he'll come around...."

"No! Please.... No...."

Her heart pounding violently, she got up and walked back to her dresser. Mechanically, she thumbed through Adam's cards until she found his driver's license.

Adam J. Ryder.

Her hands shook so hard she dropped his cards onto the dresser. She tried to swallow, but her throat was too dry. Somehow she stumbled toward the window. Outside, Paris was white rooftops and glistening, bare branches.

She dabbed wildly at her hot, wet eyes.

Adam *Jerk* Ryder was so not worth her tears!

Only when the fiend began to whistle in the kitchen was she galvanized into action. She ran to her closet and yanked clothes off hangers. Not caring if anything matched, she pulled on a pair of purple slacks and a long, red sweater.

"Breakfast is ready," he yelled. "Coffee, too. You'd better get in here while it's hot. I'm an impatient cook and I like to be complimented."

As if...

Stiff with fury, she pushed the sleeves of her red sweater up to her elbows and marched down the hall.

Somehow she had to get rid of him without giving him the satisfaction of knowing how thorough his triumph over her was.

Struggling for composure, she tiptoed into the kitchen. Everything was fine until he handed her a cup of steaming coffee and kissed her so tenderly, she began to burn for him even now when she knew who and what a low-down jerk he was.

Damn him. She swallowed and bit her lips, loathing him and herself.

"You okay? You look—"

Furious! Hurt! Crazed! All of the above, you jerk!

She pulled free of him. "I'm fine…" She bit her tongue, lowered her eyes and sipped more hot coffee.

What was his plan? To brag to Lucas?

"Coffee too strong?"

"Perfect," she said through gritted teeth. Caffeine charged through her, causing her angry heart to speed up to a truly frightening speed.

Would he tell Abigail about his little trip to Paris? Would he tell all? Or would he keep certain details to himself?

Not trusting herself to even look at him, Josie sat down and glued her eyes to the table. He set before her an omelet that looked fluffy and light.

Damn him, it was just the way she liked her omelets, too.

When he sat across from her, her stomach knotted. No way could she eat anything Adam *Jerk* Ryder had cooked.

Her fury built as he gobbled his breakfast like a man who was starving. And what man wouldn't be, after his inspired exertions in the line of brotherly duty last night? While he chopped and speared bits of omelet with truly annoying gusto, she stared at her own plate in hunger and helpless rage until the marmalade and omelet blurred into a congealed orange mass.

"So, what are you going to do with the rest of your day?" she asked, her tone dangerously soft.

"Anything you like. Make love. Or see the city. You know

Paris and its delights better than I do. You like art and gargoyles. Maybe we could walk around and admire buildings and sculpture or something…until your toes get too cold. We could come home and I could kiss them."

When he assumed she'd want to spend her day with him, and make love, a tremor went through her.

She felt his dark eyes rise from her untouched plate to her flushed, perspiring face.

"You're not sick, are you?"

She shook her head.

"Your cheeks are red, and your mouth is trembling. And your eyes…" He pushed his own plate aside and touched her wrist. "Honey, have you been crying?"

"Not over you, you thickheaded bastard!" She jerked her hand away.

He frowned. "I knew something was wrong. What the hell is it?"

Aware of his intent gaze, she clicked her nails against her mug. When his tanned hand reached across the table and covered hers, she jumped away, spilling coffee all over his wrist and arm and the table.

"Ouch!" He grabbed his burned arm. "Are you going to tell me what's eating you or not?"

"I can't do this!" she yelled.

"Do what?"

"Play your stupid games. I don't care if I burned you, okay? I'm glad, in fact! You deserve it! No, you deserve to be boiled in oil! So just get your things and go!"

"What the hell's wrong?"

"You're smart. You figure it out."

When he got up and moved toward her, she shot to her feet

so fast her chair crashed against the wall. "Don't you dare even think of ever touching me ever again—*Adam Jerk Ryder!*"

He froze. For a horrible moment the sides of his handsome face didn't seem to match up. Did he feel panic? Hurt? Remorse?

"Josie, I can explain!"

"Why bother?"

"Josie…please…"

"You heard me!" She glared at him, hating him with her entire being.

In a rage he turned and stalked to the bedroom. She heard him throwing things violently. Her heart beat faster even before he slammed back into the kitchen fully dressed.

"You went through my wallet."

"Lucas told me you didn't approve of me. You came here to get rid of me, didn't you? That's why you watched me, why you slept with me! All you ever wanted to do was to make me feel cheap and bad and ruin things for Lucas and me! Well, you succeeded!"

"No! Damn you! I would have you left alone last night! But you had to come back out and kiss me! You seduced me!"

"Oh! So this is all my fault?"

"That's not what I meant!"

She raced to her front door, intending to throw it open and demand that he leave. But when she tried to turn the difficult lock, it jammed.

When he strode over to help, she ran to her couch, watching as he flung the door so hard, it banged the wall.

"If you hadn't acted like such a damned Boy Scout, I wouldn't have let you in here last night!"

"How quickly we forget. 'Watch me,' you said. Remember that?"

Guilt ate through her like acid. "How dare you throw that up to me? Is that what you're going to tell your precious Abigail—that I made you do it?"

His eyes grew bleak. "She doesn't deserve this."

"You bastard! I don't deserve this."

"No, you don't," he whispered, his dark face agonized. "I'm sorry."

"Just get out! I don't want your apology or your pity! I hate you! I do!"

"Right. That's why you made love to me all night long!"

"Oh!"

He ripped a card out of his wallet, scribbled something on it, stalked over to the table and flung it down. "If you change your mind after you calm down, you've got all my numbers. I really hope you call me. I'd like to see you again. I'd like to explain."

"You should be very happy. You accomplished what you set out to do."

"Right. You know everything." He squared his shoulders and marched out her door.

In an attempt to act calm, she waited until she could no longer hear his footsteps before she slammed her door.

Sinking to her knees in her empty living room, she bit her lips until she tasted blood, until a painful vise squeezed the air from her lungs and cut off her breath.

She couldn't care about a man who had come to Paris solely because he thought she wasn't good enough for his family. Not when so many people before him had thought she wasn't good enough—her own mother, her stepbrothers.

Damn you, Adam Ryder! Damn you, stupid, naive Lucas, for setting me up to fall so low!

Josie dug her nails into her palms, fighting to ignore the hot tears leaking out of her eyes.

Wiping her damp cheeks with the back of her palms, Josie arose. When she saw her shade was open, she went over to her window and glanced out at his.

When she saw Adam standing motionless in his window, her heart began to thud. He looked thin and haggard, and his eyes seemed shadowed with pain.

"Bastard!"

He so didn't care! He couldn't be hurting! Not like she was! He didn't have a heart! She meant nothing to him!

Then why was he standing there, looking so dark and lost? With a cry, she ran to the window and yanked on her shade so hard, she lost her grip. The shade snapped upward, spinning around and around on its roller.

Furious, she hugged herself tightly even though he was still there, a witness to her agony.

When her phone rang, she stumbled toward it.

"Merry Christmas," Brianna said.

"I—I can't talk," Josie whispered, carrying the phone to the hall away from Adam.

"You sound really down."

"I'm fine."

"I wish you'd find somebody nice."

"*Nice*. God forbid…. I hate that word."

"Someday, it will happen for you."

"I've got to go! Bye!" Josie hung up. When she returned to the living room, Adam's window was closed and his shade was down.

She sank onto her couch. She should be happy he was gone.

Adam. Adam. Adam.

With every heartbeat, she missed him more.

Seven

Had it been nearly three weeks since Christmas? Not quite. Not yet. It just felt that long.

When Josie inserted her key into her door and kicked it, she heard a man's deep drawl as the door swung open.

"Josie, pick up! Please…"

Shivering, because it was so bitterly cold even inside her apartment and because Lucas was on her answering machine again, she hugged herself, pulling her coat tighter as she cringed against the doorjamb.

Lucas. Dear, sweet Lucas.

How many times had he called? Dozens and dozens?

He'd come by and buzzed her doorbell on the street, as well. Fortunately, Madame Picard had not been home. He'd bombarded her with e-mails, too. Not that she'd opened them.

She shut her door and locked it but did not remove her coat.
She had to get more heat going first.

"Josie, I'm com—"

What was it with the Ryder men? They just did not take a hint.

Josie swallowed at the tightness in her throat. Then she
marched toward the phone and jabbed wildly at the erase button.

Today was her first day at the gallery after the holidays. After
an interminable day, the last thing she needed was to hear the
pain in Lucas's voice. Mostly because she could not bear to
think about Adam.

All afternoon, in between checking her e-mail account and
surfing the Internet, she'd stared gloomily out at the dark,
leaden sky that had seemed to weigh the ancient city down. Her
heart had thudded with a dull, familiar pain because she missed
him so much.

If only the little brass bells on the doors had tinkled once to
signal the entrance of a customer interested in one of the bold
paintings or one of the ceramics, maybe she could have forgotten
him for a little while. But nobody had stopped at the gallery. So
her heart had continued to beat painfully and her feelings of loss
and unworthiness had built. Now she was in a truly dark mood.

Josie did not want to hurt Lucas, but Lucas was collateral
damage—because she *so* had to forget Adam.

This was not easy since Adam called and left messages
nearly every night. Not that she'd ever let herself listen to any
of them or return his calls.

Today he'd sent an e-mail to the gallery. Not that she'd
allowed herself to read it. But she'd wanted to. For ten whole
minutes her heart had thumped crazily. She'd stared at his
e-mail address, her hand on her mouse.

She hadn't been feeling well since he'd left. At first she'd simply felt "different." Then she'd come down with what she'd thought was a light case of the flu. No sooner had she gotten over that than she'd started feeling queasy or dizzy at odd times. It was not bad or often enough for her to have gone to a doctor. She chalked it up to a broken heart.

Lucas had returned to Paris January the first. Ever since, he'd relentlessly pursued her.

Determined to put both men from her mind, she went to her kitchen and lit a burner. The smell of gas made her feel queasy, but she opened her tiny refrigerator and studied her selection of cheeses, smoked fish and ham anyway.

When her stomach churned, she stood up and took a deep breath. Funny how none of it appealed to her except the sparkling water.

She twisted the cap off a bottle. As she was slicing a lemon to go in her tall fizzing glass, the ancient elevator groaned. She started when the thing stopped at her floor, and she heard heavy boots outside.

A deep muffled voice called her name. Her doorbell rang.

"Mademoiselle, you have very handsome visitor."

Lucas? Oh, no! Josie froze.

"S'il vous plaît. C'est très froid." It is very cold.

Madame knew she was home because she'd caught her on the stairs to show her some new shots of Remi.

Sure enough, when Josie turned the knob, Lucas stood in her doorway beside Madame, who was grinning from ear to ear.

"Madame said you were home. May I come in?"

She nodded. As Lucas stepped inside, Madame Picard quickly excused herself.

"Something to drink?" Unable to meet his eyes, Josie blushed. *Did he know?* "Water? Wine?"

"Neither." His voice was sharp. So were his eyes. Frowning, studying her, he tilted her chin back with a single fingertip.

Refusing to look him in the eye, she jumped back.

"Why so pale? So anxious? Are you all right?"

Maybe he did know.

She busied herself pouring glasses of wine.

He shook his head, refusing his. "How was your holiday?" She set both wineglasses down. "Great. Wonderful."

"So why haven't you returned my calls?"

"Busy." She waved a hand. "Painting."

His eyes scanned her living room and returned to her. "Where's your easel?"

No way was she going to confess that the smell of turpentine made her queasy, or that she'd procrastinated by surfing the Internet, visiting chat rooms and playing computer games.

"I went to your gallery every day, but it was always closed."

"For the holidays," she murmured.

"I finally figured that out. That's why I called you. Why I finally bribed Madame tonight."

He stared at her with such neediness, she swallowed.

So he didn't know.

"I've been awful to you, and I feel awful. I of all people know too well how badly I've made you feel. I'm sorry. But I thought you knew, that surely Adam had talked to you."

"Adam?" Lucas's lost puppy look vanished. "What's he got to do with anything?"

"So he didn't tell you that he came to Paris?"

With a look of confusion, he shook his head.

A hot rush of fury swamped her. How cruel of Adam to make her do this.

"Well, he came here over the holidays," she said.

His eyes narrowed. "Mother said he was away on business. Now that you mention it, they were both damned evasive. What the hell was he doing here anyway? With you?"

"Ask him."

Furious, hurt anew, she squared her shoulders and stalked across her living room to her window, staring defiantly out the window where she'd first spotted Adam's tall, broad-shouldered form.

Where she'd stood and lost herself in a stupid fantasy because he'd been watching.

"Fifteen days ago or so he stayed in that apartment across the courtyard," she whispered in a dull, lost tone.

"You met him?"

She nodded. "The night he arrived. His plane was late. I was hungry. We had dinner."

"What else?"

"You'll have to ask him. I shouldn't have to be the one…"

"Damn it! Look at me! Just tell me you didn't sleep with him!"

Her throat worked convulsively. Hating Adam more than ever, she turned and met Lucas's glazed eyes.

Hers probably revealed too much because his brows slashed together. Then he fisted his right hand and unfisted it.

"I'll kill him!"

Suddenly her anger was gone, and she felt very tired and lost and sad.

"I…I'm so sorry, Lucas," she said. "Really I am."

"Tell me you didn't, damn it!" He fell to his knees. "Tell me!"

"I wish…"

When she didn't deny it, he got up and ran to her, his hands gripping her shoulders, his fingers digging into her flesh. She turned away, struggling to pull loose.

Again, she went to her window and stared at the window opposite hers.

She almost expected Adam, her brutal dream lover, to materialize in those dark shadows.

Was that why she had stared out at that bleak, black rectangle nearly every night? Was she hoping to find Adam there again?

"I saw him over there. He stood in the dark watching me. I didn't know who he was—until it was too late," she said softly. "I swear! Or I would never—"

"What did you do?"

Rubbing her temples, she closed her eyes.

"You don't want to know."

"Then I'm sorry I ever met you!" His words fell like blows. "Hell. What if you're pregnant? Did you ever think of that? Or do *women like you* ever think ahead?"

So, like Adam, he saw her as someone low, someone to despise.

"I'm not pregnant!"

"Too soon to know though," he taunted, planting a seed. "You're awfully pale. I notice you didn't touch your wine."

"Go…please…."

Squeezing her eyes more tightly shut, she listened to him stomp out of her apartment and down her stone stairs. A few moments later a door slammed on the street level.

Still, she didn't move until the sudden chill and silence in her apartment made tremors go through her. When her uneasy stomach cramped, she opened her eyes and focused on her gaping door.

A gust of freezing air made her shiver.

She crossed the room and closed the door. Hugging herself because the apartment was freezing now, she sagged heavily against it.

Pregnant? How hateful of Lucas to even mention such a possibility!

Determined to eat, she stomped defiantly into her kitchen and threw open her refrigerator door.

Funny how nothing appealed to her.

Except sardines. And chocolate.

She was thirsty suddenly, but only for beer.

All her life she'd hated beer.

So, why was she suddenly having all these weird cravings?

Oh, my God…. No…. No….

Eight
<u></u>

"Two months! Have you seen a doctor?"

Brianna's dark eyes were as wide as Josie's as she studied the pregnancy test strip Josie was holding up to her pink bathroom windowpane.

"No. Madame Picard recommended somebody. I have an appointment."

"And you haven't told *him,* either?"

"I was very careful… Maybe it's just the pink morning light that's making the strip look so mauve."

Heart pounding, Josie pushed the strip even closer to the window.

"Stop trying to lie to yourself! That 'test' color band is the exact same mauve shade as the 'control' band, and you know it!"

Josie flung the strip into the trash. Sinking down on the wooden seat of her toilet, she buried her head in her hands.

"Denial. I tried to tell myself I had a stomach virus or the flu. Then the odors from the fish and poultry stalls in Montmarte started making me throw up every time I walked past them, and it got harder to lie to myself. I looked up the symptoms for first trimester on the Internet. Guess who's got every single one? Nausea. Weird cravings. Swollen breasts. Constipation."

"Okay, you've got to tell Adam! The next time he calls!"

"Right," Josie replied dully.

"Baby, I know that look. You've got to forget your pride and tell him! He can't be that bad! You said he's tried to apologize!"

"What he did was awful, humiliating! But then he made me tell Lucas. I'll never forget the hurt on Lucas's face! Maybe I'd be a hopeless romantic, too—if I had a husband like Jacques."

Talk about marrying Prince Charming. When they'd returned from their honeymoon, Jacques had surprised Brianna by installing her in a newly refurbished, eighteenth-century apartment on the Rue du Rivioli valued in excess of thirty million dollars. The apartment, which was a palace, had been in his illustrious family for centuries.

Brianna was moving up, up, up in the glamorous art world, just as she'd so longed to. Only she hadn't trapped Jacques. He'd simply appeared, like a prince in a fairy tale.

"Baby." Brianna clasped her hands in hers tightly. "Maybe this happened for a reason. Maybe everything will work out, but first you have to tell him."

"He came here because he thought I wasn't good enough to be part of his family."

"Knowing what I know, I can understand why that hurts you so much. But he didn't know you like I do, did he?"

Brianna laid her hand on Josie's flat stomach and closed her eyes. "Hey, why don't you come with me to Sainte-Chapelle, so I can pray for you?"

Protesting the whole way that she was sick at her stomach, Josie let Brianna lead her out into the city where the evening lights brightened windows as they walked beneath the leafless branches of the trees.

Brianna's arm was looped through Josie's. "I envy you your baby. Jacques and I have been trying…with no luck."

"It will happen."

"I believe that, too. Just as I believe your baby is the start of a wonderful new life for you. With or without Adam."

Without Adam. Josie fought nausea. She was still fighting it when they entered the jewel-like Sainte-Chapelle that was tucked inside the thick walls of the Palais de Justice. Wrapped within the soaring walls of red and blue stained glass, Josie let Brianna pull her down to her knees, so she could pray.

When they left the chapel a few minutes later, Josie's heart felt lighter. For the first time she wondered how her mother had felt when she'd been pregnant with her. She must have been tormented when she'd given her baby away, or she wouldn't have sent for Josie the minute her husband had died.

At least I can keep my baby even if I have to raise it alone.

That night, her oldest brother, Armand, called to tell her they'd settled with Barnardo.

"We're coming to Paris Friday to take you to dinner at the George V to celebrate. And to bring you home."

As always Armand assumed that she was his to command.

"You know the George V intimidates me."

Armand laughed without really hearing her.

"I told you before that all those place settings with all those forks and glasses…and the décor that feels like a French château…makes me feel like that awful, gauche, swamp girl you rescued."

"You should go to such places until you feel polished and relaxed."

"Now isn't a good time," she said.

"Friday," he insisted and hung up.

When her phone rang again, she grabbed it, determined to make him understand. "Armand, I can't possibly—"

"Josie? *Finally!* You answer. It's been weeks."

Adam's deep, dark voice made her melt and ache with terrifying needs.

"Josie?" Her name was a harsh demand as well as a gentle question.

"Adam?" How stupid was that? She knew who he was!

"For God's sake, are you all right?"

Her heart twisted at the desperate concern in his voice.

"I will be—as soon as I hang up on you!" Frantically, she brushed at her eyes, which stung with hot tears.

"Lucas called me. Why did you tell him about us?"

"Because you wanted me to."

"What?"

"Don't try to deny it."

"All I know is that's he's mad as hell," Adam said. "Mostly at me."

"Deservedly."

"He'll get over it. He's not why I called or have been calling. I can't quit worrying about you. I blame myself…."

"As you should."

"Are you ever going to get over being mad and listen to me?"

"Not in this lifetime."

"Do you love Lucas?"

"You," she began with icy scorn, "are the last person, the very last person, I'd ever want to share my most heartfelt feelings with."

Her hand tightened on the phone. She told herself to hang up on him. But for some reason, she couldn't.

"I guess I deserve that," he whispered in a hoarse tone that was edged with regret.

"Lucas is mad at me, too," Josie said. "He won't even speak to me. We live in the same neighborhood, and when he passes me on the street, he looks the other way. That ought to make you proud and happy, big brother. Mission accomplished."

"Do you love him?"

"None of your damn business."

"You didn't have to let him know, you know. I wasn't going to tell him."

"And we both know why—because it would hurt him more if I did the honors!"

"Hell no! Because I learned that you weren't the woman I thought you were! That you were a better woman than either of us deserved."

She clenched the phone even tighter. Did he really admire her?

She forced herself to remember how shamelessly Barnardo had flattered her before he'd betrayed her.

"Josie, look, I understand why you can't believe me right now. But if you'd just listen to me…about what happened, maybe you could make up your mind."

"I already have! What could you possibly tell me that I don't already know?"

"That I care about you. That I can't forget you. Look, I want to come to Paris to see you."

"What about Abigail?"

"Leave her out of this."

She hated the way his voice suddenly sounded so dark and strained at the mention of her name.

"I've arranged some time off because I want to see you so badly. I could be in Paris as early as this Friday."

"You big jerk! You can't have Abigail and me, too!"

"That's not—"

She'd slammed the phone down before she realized she hadn't even dropped a hint about the baby.

No way could she tell him when she was this furious.

No way.

Two days later, when the weather suddenly cleared, and the sunny afternoon became unseasonably dry and warm, Nicole, a friend of Brianna's, popped into the gallery. Tall and thin, with black hair and bright eyes, she merrily introduced herself and then demanded to see all the paintings and ceramics.

"I have some free time, so I could watch the gallery for you for a few hours," Nicole said.

"You're kidding."

"Brianna said you were a painter and that you like to walk around Paris with your camera. She said you need some time to yourself. But she's so tied up with Jacques, she can't get away. New husbands can be so demanding." She giggled. "I know mine was. But after two years, the heat is now, how you say, not so hot. But nice. Still very nice."

Nice.

Adam had been nice.

Why did everything have to remind Josie of Adam?

Nicole laughed. "I brought a book. I watch gallery before. Many times. I have key. I close the gallery for you, *non?*"

Three hours later the sun was sinking in wisps of pink clouds, and Josie was lying on the sand beneath the Eiffel Tower, her red curls flowing over the small, round disk that marked the exact center of the structure looming over her.

Grinning, she pointed her digital camera upward and snapped wildly.

Josie had spent three hours roaming Paris like a true *flâneur. Wanderer.* She still couldn't believe that she'd had an entire afternoon free to snap pictures of all the little, everyday wonders that make Paris one of the great cities of the world or that she'd felt well enough.

So, she was pregnant.

Since she was no longer in denial and feeling calmer, she could eat a few things besides chocolate and sardines. She'd even lost her taste for beer.

Her brothers were coming to celebrate the end of the Barnardo affair. Not that she was going to dine at the George V. Or tell them about the baby.

When she got up the nerve to tell Adam, maybe then she'd tell her family.

That night she felt well enough to begin a new painting of the Eiffel Tower from one of her photographs. Of course, she had to add a gargoyle or two.

She stood back and stared at her creation. Adam would want to know what it meant.

She set her paintbrush down. What did anything mean? Life was a journey without reliable tour guides. You made plans and then you got distracted and took detours that proved to be dull, disastrous, or wonderful, or a combination of all three.

She was having Adam's baby.

Adam. Longing pierced her. Strange how the pain and anger and confusion was sharper than ever—which was why she so dreaded telling him. For to do so would reopen all her needs and secret desires.

Adam. She had to find the courage to tell him.

Soon….

When Adam's phone buzzed, he frowned but kept on scribbling notes. When it buzzed the second time, he threw his pencil down.

Vanderford! He'd told her he had to get this closing statement on the Alderson land sale done by five. Ever since Paris, she knew he'd been in a race with himself to complete his time-sensitive deals. Not that she knew he planned to return to Paris ASAP.

Vanderford made it her business to keep her fingertip on his pulse. Lately when important clients had balked at being told another partner would represent them, she'd narrowed her eyes. Not that he'd told her about Josie.

When his phone buzzed again, he pushed his cuff back and glanced at his watch.

Damn. It was already four o'clock.

When she buzzed him again, he grabbed the phone and was about to growl at her, but as usual she got in the first lick.

"A Miss Brianna Boudro, sir." She hesitated. *"From Paris."*

The name *Brianna Boudro* didn't ring a bell, but he sat up straighter when she emphasized the city.

He punched a button. "Adam Ryder. Sorry to keep you waiting, Miss Boudro."

"Your secretary said you're on a tight deadline, so I'll be brief," a velvety voice purred. "We have a mutual…er, friend." As if nervous, she hesitated. "Josie…"

His hand clenched the phone in a death grip.

"*Mon dieu.* This is awkward."

His heart slammed violently. Had Josie had an accident? His lawyer's worst-case-scenario mind imagined her lying on dark, wet pavement or on a hospital bed hooked to tubes and machines.

Although the woman didn't delay all that long, Adam realized how bleak the world would be without Josie.

"She's pregnant. By you," the woman whispered.

He exploded out of his seat. His arm hit his desk so hard, the Alderson documents flew onto the carpet.

"She tells you this? And she hangs up on me? Every damn time I call her! Who the hell are you?"

"We've been best friends for years and years," she soothed. "Most recently she's run my gallery for me." Again, she hesitated. "But lately her morning sickness has been so bad, she hasn't been able to work…although she seems to be getting better."

"Does she want the baby?" He felt almost sick as he waited.

"Yes. Very much."

Adam breathed in a huge sigh of relief. "How does she plan to take care of it?"

"Her big brothers want her to come home, but she's being very indecisive. She doesn't want to tell them she's pregnant until she talks to you. She keeps saying she has to call you, but—"

"Well, damn it, why hasn't she?"

"Just call her."

"She hangs up on me every damn time I do!"

"I imagine she has her reasons."

After Brianna hung up, Adam sank back in his chair and stared blankly at the beige wall in front of him.

Vanderford chose that moment to barge in on him.

When she stared at him and then at the Alderson papers littering his carpet, he shot to his feet.

"So much for the hottest land deal in Austin," Vanderford said crisply.

They both dived for the papers. He wadded his up and flung them back onto his desk. She stacked hers neatly, stood up and placed her pile on top of his mess.

"Get Bryson. Tell him to finish the Alderson closing statement for me."

Vanderford's pencil-thin brows arched above her wire-rimmed glasses.

"Cancel all my appointments. Book me on the first available flight to Paris."

Vanderford's thin, plucked eyebrows stayed on full alert.

"Leave the return open. Then call Bob and tell him to pack a suitcase and to be on call to drive me to the airport. And, Vanderford, if you're listening, close your damn mouth."

Vanderford jumped to attention and began scribbling furiously on her notepad.

Nine

Josie had no warning that her world was about to change as she kicked her door open and let herself into her dark living room. As usual, the sofa was littered with clothes, art books and fast-food wrappers. The six bright canvasses she'd created during a whirlwind binge of painting this past week were stacked against the walls.

Setting her packages down, she glanced at her watch. In less than thirty minutes she had to be at a lecture on Chagall at the Louvre with Brianna and Jacques.

A pale, thready light slanted from the window across her picture of the Eiffel Tower with its gargoyles. The sunlight was brighter every afternoon now, which meant the days were getting longer.

She felt a curious lightness of being. Did only artists notice such things? She thought of Louisiana. Oh, how she longed for summer and sunshine and magnolia blossoms and long, hot sunny afternoons. She would be a big, fat pregnant lady by summer, and the heat would probably really wilt her. But she didn't care. She would have rented her own apartment somewhere by then, maybe in the Quarter. She'd be thinking about her baby and their future.

What about Adam?

Forgetting her date at the Louvre, she headed toward the tall window and stared up at the wispy, gray clouds before focusing on Adam's window.

The instant her gaze fell on the window, a light snapped on in his apartment. Usually the window was closed and the shade down.

Then a tall, broad-shouldered man with angular features stepped out of the shadows, her heart beat faster. His black eyes locked on her face.

"Adam?"

His eyes stripped her.

"Adam?" Her voice was a squeaky whisper. Suddenly she could barely breathe.

His hand went to his throat and unbuttoned his collar. Then his mouth moved, and she read his lips.

Watch me.

He unknotted his tie. Ripping it through his collar, he tossed it carelessly on the back of his chair. A thrilling shiver of anticipation traced through her. Then he undid the buttons of his shirt one by one until soon a strip of sleek bare chest brushed with dark hair was revealed.

Heat engulfed her.

Everything he did was blatantly sexual and possessive. Mesmerized, she began to shake.

The Louvre. The lecture. She was late.

He shrugged out of his shirt. His bare brown shoulders and well-defined, muscular arms were hard and strong. Again she remembered how safe she'd felt lying wrapped in those arms the morning after they'd made love.

She shuddered, hating herself for being so easy.

Only when he lowered his hand to the button at his waistband above his swollen fly, did she summon a shred of gumption.

Reaching up, she yanked her shade down. Then she spun on her heel and ran to her bedroom. Throwing herself onto her bed, she fought to ignore the zing of hot sensuality still thrumming in her veins.

Her cell phone began to ring. Furious at him for tempting her, she grabbed it only to gasp when she saw Adam's number in vivid blue.

She answered and then hung up on him. Immediately she punched in Brianna's number.

"*He's here!* Did you tell him? Tell me you didn't!"

"This could be a good thing." Brianna's voice was a shade shy of a whisper. "You said you didn't want to go back to New Orleans to your family until you told him. This is not just *your* problem. It's *his,* too."

"Listen to me. Just because you're floating in happily-ever-after clouds, this is not true love like you and Jacques—"

"No, you listen. Give the man a chance! Give *yourself* a chance!"

"I wish I'd never told you!"

Immediately after hanging up on Brianna, Josie's cell phone vibrated again. Adam again.

A man like Adam, who'd come all the way to Paris because

he'd gotten her pregnant, wasn't going to stop harassing her until she, at least, talked to him.

"Adam?"

"I know about the baby." His voice was hard and dark and held zero sympathy.

Tears stung her eyes. "Not your concern." Even as she said it, she knew how ridiculous she sounded.

"We need to talk."

"If you think I'm going to let you bully me the way you bully Lucas…"

"I'm coming over to discuss options."

"Not tonight! I'm going out. To a lecture at the Louvre. On contemporary art. Chagall."

"I'll take you."

"I'm meeting friends."

"So? I'll be at your place in five minutes. If you don't open the door, I will inform Madame Picard you're pregnant with my child and I'm worried about you. I'll call the police and tell them the same thing."

"No! No! No!"

She wanted to wear something nicer than the black sweater and skirt and bangles she'd worn all day. But there was no time to change.

Blind with panic, she grabbed her coat and ran out the door, only to slam straight into Adam's tall, heavy-shouldered body.

When she screamed, he caught her to him and laughed.

She broke loose and tried to scramble back into her apartment and slam the door, but he stuck his long, polished boot inside it, grabbed her arms and scooped her easily against the solid expanse of his body again.

She caught the faintest trace of his aftershave. He smelled

good. He felt good. Instantly her heart began to race at a shameful pace.

"Damn you," she said even as her fingers were furrowing into his thick hair. The thing she hated most was how glad she was to see him.

"Damn you, too," he muttered thickly, but he pulled her closer and buried his head in her collar for a long moment. Maybe he liked holding her, too.

"Let me go," she whispered.

"Only if you promise not to make me chase you."

She nodded weakly. "Okay. Anything… Just take your hands off me."

As always, he was so big, he seemed to dominate her tiny, cluttered apartment.

He studied her paintings without commenting on them. Then he turned back to her. "So, we've got a date to the Louvre? Like any normal couple?"

She grabbed her black bag. "We are so *not* a normal couple!"

"Maybe we should become one. After all, you're having my baby."

"It would never work." The thought made her eyes shiny.

"Not if you fight me every step of the way."

"What else can I do when you think Ryders are royalty and way too good for a woman as low as me?"

"Shut up about that. Just shut up. Beliefs aren't set in stone. People can change—for good or bad—if they want to badly enough. For the record, I don't think you're low. I came as soon as I heard you were pregnant with my child."

She heaved in a breath. "I don't believe you."

"I don't care whether or not you believe me—it's the truth! And I'm not going home until we hash out a deal."

"So this is just a business arrangement to you." She marched toward her front door.

"No. I care about you and the baby. I'm here to help."

"The last thing I want is you taking over my life."

"You should have thought of that before you became pregnant with my child. Maybe I should have been a helluva lot more careful, too. Look, you and I are in this mess together—for better or worse, as they say." His voice softened. "I say we figure out how to make the best of it!"

Ten

Do we really look like any other normal couple? Josie wondered as they stood beneath architect I. M. Pei's brilliantly lit glass pyramid.

Could they ever *be* a normal couple?

Holding her museum map while Adam studied his, Josie glanced anywhere but at him as passersby rushed past them.

Adam jabbed his finger at Chagall's portrait on her map. "Weird. I see why the Russians threw him out."

She jumped at his bait. "That's all you have to say about Chagall's genius?"

He grinned down at her. It annoyed her that he was so happy at having manipulated her into anger so easily.

He pointed toward the escalator. "What do you say we skip the lecture and head for the Egyptian antiquities?"

The teasing glint in his eyes told her he wanted an argument.

She wanted to give him one, too, but if they went to the lecture, Brianna, who was on his side, would take charge. Thus, when Adam touched her elbow, she meekly nodded and then let him steer her toward the escalator.

"How can I even talk to someone who has zero appreciation for artistic genius?" she grumbled.

"It doesn't bother me that you probably don't appreciate the finer technicalities of Texas law regarding real estate," he replied easily.

"You are so not funny."

"I thought I'd try an icebreaker or two before I got down to discussing the terms of our quickie marriage."

"Quickie marriage?"

"And our flight home to Louisiana and Texas to inform our families."

"Did you just propose to me? Here?"

"Do you want me to get down on bended knee? Here?"

When he stopped in midstride to kneel, she would have kicked him if he hadn't jumped back out of her range.

"My mother, for one, er…once she gets over the shock, will be thrilled to be a grandmother," he said. "She'd about given up on me. How about yours?"

"She will be too mortified for words."

"Unless you're Mrs. Adam J. Ryder."

"No!"

"Trust me." He seemed about to say more, but thought better of it, maybe because he saw how angry she was.

Pointing down a corridor, he took off at a brisk pace instead, leading her through vast, mazelike rooms.

"We can't just get married," she said. "We barely know each other."

"You're pregnant."

"I can't marry a man who doesn't love me, whose only reason for sleeping with me was to make his brother dislike me."

"If you would ever listen, you'd know that's not why I slept with you."

"Do you deny that you came here because you wanted to ruin things between Lucas and me?"

"All right. Believe whatever you want! This isn't about us...or Lucas or what we want anymore."

"And Abigail?"

"I don't want to talk about her—ever. You're pregnant, damn it. We're going to have a child. That's all that matters."

His cold gaze flicked to his map. Like a hunter, he scanned their surroundings and pointed. "That way."

He grabbed her by the hand and led her through a door. Suddenly they were inside a vast room with high ceilings. Immense, awe-inspiring Egyptian statues frowned down at them.

He scowled up at a statue. "Impressive."

She glanced at the stern likenesses of pharaohs and their queens, then back at him.

"Abigail's the kind of wife you really want."

"Discussing her now is pointless."

When Josie touched his hand, he jerked away.

"I was just trying to say that times have changed," she said. "I don't want to trap you. You can still marry her."

"What? And leave you here, pregnant? Or worse, let you go home to New Orleans pregnant and alone...to a family who'd be ashamed of you and my child if you weren't married? Do you want your child to feel unwanted...the way you did?"

The breath went out of her. Sensing his advantage, he moved closer, backing her against a wall. "I can't just forget my child…or you. Not when you have dark circles under your eyes. Not when you can't work, and you're ill a lot. Hell, you're barely taking adequate care of yourself now. When the baby comes, what will you do then? I want to help you. Please, let me."

"I have morning sickness, which is perfectly normal under the circumstances. As soon as it stops, I'll be fine."

"Maybe. Maybe not. I hope so. But either way I want to take care of you while you're pregnant. Why is that so awful?"

"Because we're strangers. Because I'm not your concern."

"You're three months along with my child. Look, I'm not exactly happy about this, either. Or proud of the way I behaved. But I don't want to go on playing the bastard. It's not like we'd have to stay married forever. We could marry for, say, nine months. After the baby's strong and healthy, you can have your freedom again. And so can I."

"But that's crazy," she cried. "It wouldn't be a real marriage."

When a group of schoolgirls turned and stared at them, he frowned.

"You hungry?" he said in a lower tone.

"What?"

"Is there a café nearby where we could talk…without making a scene?"

She nodded. "Yes, but it's a bit of a walk."

They didn't speak on the way to the brightly lit café. Once there they selected fruit crepes. After he ordered wine and she coffee, he carried both their trays and arranged their food on a little table beside a charming fountain surrounded by statues and plants.

"So, we'd have a temporary marriage." He pulled out a chair for her and then sat down across from her. "I have a huge house. And money. How difficult can it be for two civilized people to live together for nine months?"

She shut eyes. He felt nothing for her other than obligation. Why couldn't he understand how that might hurt?

"Maybe we could even become friends," he said.

"Friends?" She almost choked because she wanted so much more but had to deny all her true feelings.

"All right." His face darkened. "Forget the friend part. I can't blame you for disliking me."

"I don't dislike you," she whispered.

"Well, you damn sure don't like me." He ran a hand through his hair. "Look, I'm a lawyer. I work all the time. I could volunteer for a lot of the firm's out-of-town assignments. You'd hardly ever have to see me. Even when I stayed home, you could have your own floor of the house. Hell, you could do whatever you want—drive a nice car, order pizza in…. I swear, I'll stay the hell out of your way if you'll just marry me and give my child my name."

"I don't like pizza." Her voice broke plaintively.

"I was just using pizza as an example." He pulled his chair back and stared up at the ceiling.

His dark eyes were glassy. He looked so tired, she felt sorry for him. She almost reached across the table to brush a fingertip across his hand.

"Okay, crepes, sardines, tuna, whatever," he muttered, lowering his head and gazing at her.

"Sardines?" She fought the urge to smile. "How did you know about my weird craving?"

"You almost drooled over the sardines and herring in the line a while ago."

His voice had softened in that way that made her melt, so she kept her gaze fixed on one of her moon-shaped wedges of cantaloupe.

"You're very observant. You notice and remember everything I do or say."

"I'm a lawyer. It goes with the territory." He sighed wearily. "You could shop…paint. I have a live-in, a man—Bob. He takes care of the house. You wouldn't have to cook or clean. In fact Bob is too territorial for that. He won't *let* you cook or clean. Heaven help you if you try. Hell, he damn near chopped one of my fingers off when I opened a jar of peanuts in the kitchen the other night."

She grinned. "Bob? He sounds unusual."

"He's a character, all right. I won't worry about you with him there to see after you."

"I can't believe I'm actually listening to you say all this, like it could really happen."

"It could. It will if you'll let it. And afterward—when you are on your feet and the baby's three months old and you go your way, and I go mine—I'll want to remain part of the baby's life."

Despair over their inevitable parting caused her to draw a deep, painful breath. Losing him once had been unbearable. Losing him after being married to him, after watching him hold their baby… How would she stand it?

"I'm willing to be very generous financially—during and after the marriage," he said.

Nervously she stacked her little white plates and then unstacked them. "I understand. *Money.* Of course, you think that's all I care about…."

"Damn it, don't put words in my mouth!"

"I'm sorry."

"Maybe you're right that I'm a hard-hearted monster. But for the baby, don't you think we should try to work together? Josie, I really want to help. This isn't the only mistake I've ever made in my life, you know. This time I want to do the right thing. I will, if you'll let me."

When she restacked their plates again, he grabbed a plate from her and set it down firmly. "It would only be for nine months. That's not so long. Just think about it."

"I don't want to marry you." Knotting her napkin tightly, she threw it on her stack of dishes. "Not for nine months. Not for one day."

Dark emotion flared in the icy depths of his eyes. Anger? Hurt? Whatever it was, some part of her wished she could modify what she'd said.

"Okay. Let's talk about exactly what my money could do for you. Security for your baby. Free room and board. A studio of your own. Freedom to paint as much as you want for nine months. And, best of all, a lump sum when we divorce. All we have to do is decide on the amount of that final settlement."

Feeling queasy, she pushed away from the table. "I need some air." Spotting the ladies' room, she ran toward it, not because she needed to use it. She simply needed to get away from him.

"How much?" he demanded.

Goaded, she whirled. "How much? You want to know how much? Maybe I'm not for sale!"

She flung the door open and ran into the closest stall. She closed the door and stood there until she felt calm. Then she washed her hands and face. She was still wiping her forehead with cold towels when a French woman with a cherubic face and tight, white curls, said a man outside was worried about her.

"Tell him I'm fine."

When Josie finally stepped out into the hall, Adam's face was alarmingly dark, and his eyes were filled with concern. "Are you really all right?"

"Can we go home?" she whispered. "I'm tired. Really tired."

"I'm sorry I upset you."

She didn't speak until they were outside the museum and the cool, damp air revived her.

"Why don't we walk?" she said.

"Are you crazy?" When he spotted a cab, he stepped into the street and held up his hand.

The ancient vehicle that stopped reeked so strongly of cigarettes and red wine, she had to open the window. The driver had a long gray beard and ponytail and a cynical fascination for French politics. When he started ranting about the communists, he slammed his foot down onto the accelerator. She forgot her fear of Adam. In fact she clung to him as the lunatic at the wheel sped faster and faster through the damp, dark streets.

Only when their cabbie pulled up to their building did she let go of his arm. While Adam was paying the bill, she would have run up the stairs if he hadn't read her mind and held on to her arm. When he was done with the cabbie, he led her to the elevator.

Shaking her head, she pointed to the stairs.

"You're too tired."

"I'm claustrophobic."

He pulled her inside. "Then shut your eyes and hold on to me."

His touch was oddly reassuring, which was completely illogical. He was heavy. He added weight. He took up room.

The doors closed, and the elevator rumbled and jerked slowly up to her floor.

"Hell," he said. "This thing's enough to give *me* claustrophobia. I should have carried you up the stairs."

"Maybe next time."

The elevator made a shrieking sound and fell a foot before

it bounced to a stop. She held her breath until it began to climb again. Imagining the walls squeezing in upon her, she kept her eyes shut and her body pressed against Adam.

The elevator screamed and bounced again, jostling their bodies more tightly together.

"Definitely next time," he growled. "This is hell."

"I told you so, didn't I?"

"At least we're together."

"Yes." Strangely, she was comforted by his nearness.

Eleven

When the cage bumped hard at the second floor, Adam was holding her close, and she was grinding her face into his shoulder.

Finally, the thing stopped and the doors actually opened. Even after they leapt to safety, she clung to him and was glad when he kept his arm around her as he pried her key from her shaking fingers, so he could open her door.

Shrugging out of his leather jacket as he followed her inside, he closed her door.

"Okay, then…" Without meeting her eyes, he began to pace. "I say we finish this unpleasant business, so we can move on."

When he hesitated, something in his hard look made her tense.

"So, how much of a settlement do you want?"

Money. Again? She wanted to scream, to pound his thick chest, his even thicker head. Instead, she sank down on her couch and buried her head in her hands.

"Money? Do you really think me so low that you think that's all I care about?"

"This isn't a moral issue. Think of it as math."

"Never my favorite subject."

"How much?"

Furious, exhausted, she closed her eyes. "All right!"

With a hoarse whisper she named an outrageously high sum.

He hissed in a breath. "Well, I damn sure underestimated you. But okay. You'll get what you want, as long as I get what I want—a chance to know my child."

Her eyes snapped open again. His face was dark and hard; his black eyes drilled her.

"I'll have the papers drawn up at once. When we divorce, I'll write the check. Oh. One more thing." His voice was so shivery soft, she trembled. "A final detail."

He knelt before her. Gently he took her hand. Turning it palm-up, he lifted it to his lips as a lover would to a woman he truly wished to marry. Diamonds and sapphires flashed as he slid a ring onto her finger.

With a little gasp, she looked from him to the diamonds and sapphires twinkling on her left hand.

"It fits perfectly," he said. "I don't know about you, but I could use a good omen."

In the hush that fell, her eyes filled with tears.

"It's exquisite," she whispered. "No one has ever…" She broke off, not wanting him to know how touched and vulnerable she felt.

Josie's bruised heart contracted painfully. Had he chosen it for her? Or for Abigail?

"Nobody is to know this is a temporary arrangement," he said. "For the baby's sake, I want my family and yours to think we loved each other at least for a little while. So when we're around other people, we'll act like we love each other. To the world we have a real marriage."

"For the baby's sake," she whispered. She was shaking so much, the ring shot sparks.

She swallowed. *No problem. I won't even have to lie. 'Cause, me, stupid me, I love you.*

She lowered her lashes, so he couldn't see that her eyes had filled with tears. "No sex," she said in a low tone.

His breath quickened, searing her cheek and throat and causing her to ache with bittersweet longing.

"Separate beds." She stared stupidly past him to her easel.

Furious, he shot to his feet.

"Separate bedrooms!" she whispered.

"Suit yourself." His voice cut like ice. "Separate wings if you wish."

"Separate houses! That's what I wish! I wish I'd never met you!"

"Do you?" He turned.

Suddenly, before she knew what he intended, he seized her wrists and yanked her up. When he snapped her against his body, she shrieked in outrage even as some true, dark part of her thrilled to his embrace.

"Is that what you really feel?" His mouth was dangerously close to hers. "I wonder."

"I'll tell you how I feel!" She jabbed his chest with her elbows, half a dozen ill-conceived insults learned in a forgotten swamp spewing out of her lips.

"Well, I damn sure can't delude myself that I'm marrying a lady after that. Not that I ever wanted you to be a lady in bed."

With a squeal of fury, she broke off in the middle of a vivid curse.

"So you hate me, do you?" His eyes darkened. Then his mouth slanted across hers in a scorching kiss.

Her lips fused to his, she twisted and kicked, but her struggles merely caused him to tighten his grip. When she opened her mouth to cry for help, his hot tongue invaded her lips.

One kiss and the shameful heat she wanted to deny began to build, until it nearly consumed her. The sinful, devouring kiss went on and on until soon that secret part of her that was his willed him never to stop.

His kiss held more than a question, more than the will to dominate. Fierce and greedy, his passion ignited hers, causing a dizzying, melting weakness to spread throughout her body. When he released her wrists, she slid her arms around his neck. With a triumphant cry, he ground his body into hers and deepened the kiss, which was all it took for the last of her resistance to ebb into nothingness.

Her lips left his mouth to brush the hollow of his throat. "Adam. Oh, Adam…"

In the next second his hard arms sent her tumbling backward onto her couch. Then his long body was sprawled on top of hers.

"Ouch!"

"Did I hurt you?"

"No. My art books!"

Gently he pulled her to her feet and swept her big art books and clutter onto the floor. When she kissed him, he smiled and lowered her again, following her down.

His knee pushed, opening her thighs, and she sighed with pleasure when she felt the pressure of his hot, blatant arousal against her belly.

"Too many clothes," he said in a low, hoarse undertone that was somehow frightening because of its intensity.

"No…"

But when his mouth covered hers again, she couldn't stop kissing him back.

"No…yes…yes…yes. Oh, *yes!*"

He wound his fingers through her hair. Her hands circled his neck, sliding into his thick hair as well.

"Yes," she purred, "Oh, yes…"

"I thought so."

When her nails sank into the back of his neck, he grinned. "Now I know so."

Forcing himself to turn away, he expelled a breath that ripped through him on a harsh shudder. Then his whole body went rigid.

He grimaced as if in pain. Then he forced his hands to fall away from her. With a groan he pushed himself up and off her.

With hands that shook he smoothed her skirt back over her thighs and arranged her legs in a more modest pose. After that he just sat there, at the end of her couch, breathing hard, staring into space, fighting for control.

When, at last, his breath grew more regular, he finger-combed his black hair. With equal deliberation, he straightened his tie.

"What?" she whispered. "What's wrong?"

With a frown, he leaned over her. "As if you can't guess." Pressing a fingertip to her mouth, he gently traced the shape of her full, lower lip.

Confused, she shook her head. "I can't."

"You're very beautiful, but I think things are complicated enough between us right now. The last thing we need is more sex."

"You don't want me?"

"You said no sex. Separate bedrooms? We made a deal."

She shook her head, not wanting any of that now.

With a heavy sigh, he said, "Be happy. I'm giving you exactly what you want."

Feeling anything but happy, she swallowed.

"Something in me snapped a while ago. Look, I just pounced. I guess those are the feelings that got us into this lousy mess in the first place. Once we marry, if I'm to stay out of your bed, *as you wish,* I'll definitely need to work out of town a lot."

But what if I don't wish?

He seemed to sense the new tension inside her. "Look, you said you were tired. I show up out of the blue tonight and make all these demands. Maybe I've pressured you enough for one night."

"But what if I—I…want…"

He was standing up, when she laid a tentative hand on top of his and stroked his long fingers.

He froze. Feeling rejected, she jerked her hand from his quickly.

"I'll see you tomorrow morning," he said quietly, firmly.

Feeling miserable, she nodded.

He got up and grabbed his jacket and flung it over his wide shoulder. "Tomorrow, we'll begin making the necessary arrangements."

Necessary arrangements? How cold and unromantic that sounded. Like any girl she'd dreamed of planning her fairy-tale wedding.

"You make them," she whispered.

"All right then."

Without a backward glance, he strode out her door, slamming it so hard, she felt as if he'd slapped her.

"Better lock it," he yelled as if he were already her husband with rights to order her around.

His racing footsteps resounded loudly in the stone stairwell. Would he have run so eagerly from Abigail?

Twelve

The hour was early. Sainte-Chapelle was strangely hushed and felt unbearably sacred, at least to Josie.

Stained glass sparkled like jewel-colored tears on all sides of her. Forcing a smile, Josie fought to ignore the cold knot of fear in her stomach as she gripped Adam's arm tightly.

Their wedding, which Adam had arranged, was so perfect it would have brought tears to Josie's eyes, if only he loved her.

He'd made the *necessary* arrangements. That was all.

The priest, who was to marry them, was tall and gaunt. His solemn, disapproving eyes seemed able to read every doubt in her uncertain soul. As if he sensed her fears, or maybe he had his own, Adam's hand tensed around hers.

When the priest finally lowered his gaze to his Bible and began speaking French, Josie's heart was pounding so fiercely, she couldn't understand a single word.

What they were doing was wrong. So wrong. Adam didn't love her, and he never would.

Suddenly it seemed cruel that he'd given her such a beautiful ring. Cruel that he'd paid to have her hair styled. Cruel that he'd bought her the off-white designer gown and veil that had made her so breathless when she'd first seen it in a couturier's window last week.

With Adam at her side, the designer and his assistants had treated her like a princess. She'd twirled around and around in the dress. Full of pride and gaiety, she'd tilted her head back and laughed.

When Adam's eyes had met hers in the mirror, his tanned face had softened. "You look beautiful."

He'd held up his hand, snapping his fingers. In an instant Josie was surrounded by seamstresses.

Eight hours later an enormous gold package had arrived at her apartment. She'd opened it and unfolded the tissue, her vision blurred as she lifted the hastily altered gown.

Why was he marrying her here, in her favorite chapel, in this fairy-tale dress?

When she'd asked Brianna if she'd suggested the chapel and the dress, Brianna's large, almond eyes had twinkled.

"Maybe he loves you."

If only she could confide in Brianna and tell her that the marriage wasn't real, and that the nicer he was, the more painful it would be for her when he divorced her.

He'd been too nice this past week. When he hadn't been cooking or caring for her, he'd been on the phone, making arrangements for their wedding and for her move. Insisting that she rest, he'd shopped, buying mostly organic food. He'd hired movers and had packed most of her things himself.

One night after they'd dined on baked chicken, steamed broccoli and a baked potato, he'd apologized for his rudimentary cooking skills.

"I ate it all, didn't I?"

If only they'd been a real couple, she might have taken his hand or kissed him. She might have slowly placed his hand to her stomach and held it there. But not once in the past week had he touched her or tried to kiss her again, so she'd behaved coolly and impersonally, too.

The priest asked her if she took Adam to be her husband. In hushed tones that echoed, she looked into Adam's eyes and said yes. On a deep, shuddering note Adam pressed her hand, brought it to his lips and promised himself to her forever.

Brianna and Jacques, Madame Picard and a sullen Lucas were their only witnesses. When Adam had told her Lucas was coming, she'd been startled.

"But Lucas is so unhappy about this. Why do you want him at our wedding?"

"So he can know that you belong only to me."

During the wedding Lucas gazed at the stained glass windows.

When it was time for Adam to kiss her, his lips grazed hers swiftly. Then he whispered against her ear. "We have a plane to catch."

No reception was planned. Seconds later, he pulled her toward the nearest exit.

Outside, beneath gray skies, Lucas looked even more relieved than his brother to have it over. With a curt nod at her, he shook his brother's hand, waved to the others and was off.

Madame, however, embraced Josie, kissing her twice on both cheeks. Then she turned to Adam and kissed him with equal passion.

"I must be gone. To catch train. To see Remi." Of course, she couldn't leave without showing everybody her latest snapshots of her darling grandson.

"He has my eyes, *non?*"

When raindrops began to pelt them, Adam helped Josie into the stretch limo that was parked on the curb.

Silk skirts rustling, she twisted around to wave to Brianna and Jacques. Long after the limousine had rounded a corner and Brianna was no longer visible, Josie continued to stare out the back window.

"Fasten your seat belt," Adam whispered.

"Because of the baby?"

"Just do it."

Feeling both apprehensive and light-headed, she sank back against the leather seat.

"Why can't we live apart?" she whispered. "Why are you forcing me to live with you?"

"We're married. You're my wife and my responsibility now. Along with the child."

"The baby. Always the baby."

"Yes, the baby. *Our* baby."

"Adam?" She hesitated. "There's something I haven't told you…."

All week she'd tried not to think about the jet's cabin door shutting them inside, about how trapped and helpless she'd felt when she'd flown over before, and then she'd had medication. She didn't want him to see her at her worst, to think the worst of her.

"I—I…I'm a very nervous flyer," she admitted. "Usually, I take a pill."

"But you can't today…because of the baby."

"Yes."

His warm fingers curled over hers reassuringly. "It'll be all right."

She hoped so. She didn't want to embarrass him.

Since they were in first class, Josie was clutching her armrest and staring out the open door at the gray sky. At least they weren't shut in yet.

Not that that was all that was bothering her.

"New Orleans? We're going to New Orleans? You could have at least told me."

Adam thrust his briefcase under the seat in front of him and unfolded his newspaper. "You did tell me to make all the arrangements. Whenever I so much as asked you a question, you gave me the silent treatment."

"Still, you should have told me."

"I'm telling you now."

"So this is how it's going to be."

"I know how nervous you are, but I prefer not to make scenes in public places." He shot a glance at the passengers filing past them.

"And my family? Did you inform them, too?"

"Your brothers are picking us up at the airport."

"They're in on this, too! Why am I surprised?"

"As your husband, I need to meet your family at some point." He snapped open his newspaper. "New Orleans is on the way. We'll only be there a day. Maybe next time you'll be more willing to help me plan…."

"How dare you blame this on…on me!"

When the pretty flight attendant serving first class came to take their drink order, Josie bit back the rest of her retort. Her frown gave way to a smile. "Coffee, please. Decaf. Sugar."

Adam's newspaper rattled ominously.

"Something for you, too, sir?"

He lowered his paper and shook his head. The pretty flight attendant scampered away. The door shut, and the flight attendant asked that all electronics be turned off.

Josie gulped in several breaths. Suddenly a fight seemed infinitely preferable to terror.

"Maybe I don't want you to meet my family. Maybe since this isn't a real marriage, I don't want you in my real life."

"Our marriage *is* real. At least for the next nine months!"

"Nine months? You call that a marriage?"

"You'll be meeting my family soon, too."

"I didn't want to involve my family."

"We're having a baby. They're all going to be grandparents."

"Oh, so you told them about the baby, too?"

"I thought you might want to do that."

"I'm stunned by your insight."

"Finally. You're pleased about something I've done. Anything else? Or are you going to deal with your panic attack like an adult—without abusing me? I'd like to read my paper in peace."

When he raised his paper, she felt shut out. This should have pleased her, but, of course, it didn't. When her coffee arrived, she was so furious, she pushed it aside.

Naturally, the flight attendant returned and wanted to know if anything was wrong. Josie shook her head.

The stewardess's gaze slid from Josie to Adam, who was mostly hidden behind his newspaper. He still wore his elegant suit while Josie had brushed out her bridal hairdo and had pulled it up in a little knot from which red curls dripped messily.

She'd put on her oldest, paint-spattered jeans, a comfy gray sweater and lots of jingly bangles because such clothes made her feel relaxed. They probably looked like the most mis-matched couple in the universe.

"What beautiful wedding rings." The woman's soft voice was filled with genuine admiration.

"We just got married." Feeling embarrassed, Josie hid her left hand behind her.

"Congratulations! That's so thrilling!"

Adam's muscular arm tensed. "I'll have a whiskey," he growled. "On the rocks. Make it a double."

"Right away, sir."

"Good, I've driven you to drink," Josie said.

"And it isn't even noon." He snapped his paper open again. "That's a first."

"Good!"

"Get a grip!"

The jet was roaring down the runway. Not that Josie was afraid as her fingers clawed her armrests. She was too annoyed at Adam.

Fully intending to stay mad at him forever, or at least until the jet's landing gear hit solid tarmac, she sulkily sank lower in her own seat. But the steady hum of the jet engines soothed her and made her drowsy, and soon, despite her usual fears, she was asleep. She might have stayed that way for the entire flight if the plane hadn't hit turbulence.

The jet dived into nothingness, and she screamed.

Adam's arms closed around her instantly. "Bad dream?"

She nodded. Vaguely she remembered white alligators chasing her, but they weren't nearly as scary as finding herself trapped with Adam inside a falling jet. Not that he didn't feel strong and protective beside her.

"It's going to be okay," he murmured. "I promise."

The cabin was dark and hushed now. Adam removed his earphones and turned his attention from his movie to her. She yanked her head off his shoulder and tried to push away his muscular arm, which was draped around her.

Stiffening, she sat up and pulled her armrest down, to separate his body from hers.

"Sure that's what you want?" He shot her a superior smile.

"You are so annoyingly conceited," she began.

The jet, which had to be on *his* side, hit an air pocket and plunged, causing her to cry out and grab him.

"I told you so." With a broad smile, he pulled her back into his arms and pressed his lips into her hair. "There, there. Nothing to worry about."

"*Nothing to worry about?* How can you keep saying that?"

"Statistics show—"

"I've seen too much footage of burning plane wreckage! Jets are as flimsy as eggshells!"

"If you don't stop it, you're going to scare me! Then who's going to comfort you?"

Maybe he did have a teeny-weeny point.

She bit her tongue and let him hold her. When his lips touched her hair again, they felt so warm and nice, she almost shivered with pleasure. When the jet hit more rough air and hurtled downward, she would have snuggled even closer, except his armrest jabbed her breast.

"Ouch!"

"Told you so!" With a smile, he lifted the armrest.

She threw herself into his arms, plastering herself to him.

"That's better," he whispered. "Who knows? A couple of more bumpy flights, and you may fall head over heels in love with me."

"No way! As soon as I get on the ground…"

"Then hush, so I can enjoy what's left of the flight."

Thirteen

"**Y**ou two will be in the red room," Gigi, Josie's mother, said as she glided into the parlor.

"My old room?" Every muscle in Josie's body tensed at the thought of sharing her tiny, intimate bedroom with Adam.

"Dinner's almost ready. Why don't you show Adam upstairs so he can freshen up?"

Before Josie could protest, Adam sprang to his feet.

Since meeting Adam, her slim, youthful mother had been on her best behavior. Chattering gaily about "those awful" Union officers who'd ridden their war horses inside the house during the Civil War, she led Adam out into the hall.

"Stallions! Why, those mean ol' lieutenants tore up everything with their sabers and spurs. Thought we had gold hidden, and, of course, we did."

Adam excused himself briefly to get their suitcases, which

Armand had left beneath an affable portrait of Robert E. Lee in the grand entranceway.

Looking very pleased, Gigi laid a smooth, white hand on the banister and waited for him. She remained there, watching proudly as Josie led him up the beautiful, curved, marble stairway.

The house, a magnificent Greek Revival double-galleried mansion, had been in Gigi's family for generations. Surrounded by century-old magnolias, oaks and azaleas, the home was a favorite with tourists who visited the Garden District.

When Josie reached her bedroom door, she froze.

"Excuse me," Adam said, brushing past her with their bags.

Gathering her courage, she ran inside and threw open the shutters, forcing herself to focus on the green garden below where she and Brianna used to sketch. The last thing she wanted to look at was the narrow four-poster bed that she'd slept in as a young girl.

When Adam dropped their suitcases on the plush, rose-patterned carpet with a thud, she jumped.

"Delightful room," he said behind her.

"Yes, but we did agree on separate bedrooms."

The zipper of his suitcase sounded like an angry explosion when he ripped his bag apart. When she turned, he was on his knees rustling through his things.

"So what do you call this thing with the red bedspread on it in the middle of the room?"

Was that low growl a curse he muttered under his breath?

He stood up slowly, a cynical, half smile twisting his hard mouth. His appraising gaze roamed her body from head to toe. Then he studied the tiny red bed.

"A double bed. *Yours,* I believe."

"An old-timey, *little, very little* double bed. Hardly big enough for me alone. I should know."

Adam shrugged. "Antiques, I believe they call them. Not the most comfortable furniture in my book, but your mother does seem to have an affinity for them."

Her hand fell from the shutter. "We made a bargain. You've got to do something."

"You want me to tell your mother we want separate bedrooms? On our wedding night? When we agreed to pretend this is a real marriage?"

"So…tell her we'd prefer a hotel."

"You saw how excited she was at the airport. She's gone to a lot of trouble."

"I thought it was sickening the way everybody fawned all over you."

"It's called Southern hospitality. They were only being nice to me because they love you."

She remembered how they'd looked at her so silently and judgmentally when they'd first brought her here. How they'd made her stand on the veranda, how her mother had lifted her hands and inspected her torn, black fingernails, wondering aloud if they'd ever come clean.

"You're not jealous?" His voice softened. So did his eyes. "Is that it?"

She shrugged with an air of indifference. No way could she admit how she'd longed for them to welcome her home as they had welcomed him tonight. But they'd never accepted *her*…until she'd brought him home.

"Don't be jealous," he said. "They were nice to me because they *love* you."

"But our marriage isn't real."

"Do you remember the prenup we signed?" His expression darkened, and she remembered how awful she'd felt, knowing she wasn't the kind of woman he'd ever marry unless he'd had to, when she'd watched him sign it.

"It's legal as hell," he said. "And real."

"Until you, I don't think I've ever done one thing that's pleased them," she whispered.

"I'm sure you're wrong."

"How would you know? Your family probably puts you on a pedestal."

"Okay. I don't know…now. Maybe someday, you'll tell me."

"*Someday?* How can you speak as if we actually were a normal couple who have a real future? As if you'd care…."

"Okay. Hell, stick with your doomsday scenario about us and our future. As for now, this minute, what do you think we're accomplishing with this conversation? Look, the flight was rough on you. We're both tired. Why don't we both just shut up and get ready for dinner? Hey, maybe you'd feel better about yourself if you changed…."

"If *I* changed?" She tensed defensively. "So you disapprove of what I'm wearing, too?"

His expression gentled. "I don't think your mother's the denim type."

While her mother had been thrilled with Adam in his elegant suit, her mouth had tightened at Josie in her paint-spattered jeans. Not that she'd said anything…*then*.

No, she'd waited until they'd been alone in Armand's car waiting for the men to bring the luggage.

"How did a girl like you ever catch a man like Adam?"

Instantly, Josie had been reduced to that dirty, unwanted, thirteen-year-old swamp child on the veranda.

Adam zipped his suitcase shut, and the sound sliced through Josie's tissue-thin ego like a knife.

"She probably puts too much emphasis on appearances," he said. "And you probably dress like that to annoy her."

"You don't know why I—"

"This isn't just about you. She spent all day cooking dinner. To honor us…and our marriage."

"All right. Agreed. But what about later…tonight? *The bed?*"

He went over to the bed and laid a large, brown hand on the gleaming satin spread. "I say we make the best of things."

"You would. You're a man."

"What the hell is that supposed to mean?"

His gaze caught hers and held it. "Do you really think I can't share a bed with you and keep my hands to myself?" he demanded roughly.

"I…I…"

Tracking her, he sprang across the tiny bedroom, his long strides falling silently in the deep pile of the carpet. She skittered backward, stopping abruptly when her shoulders hit the wall.

Towering over her, he raised a hand on either side of her, trapping her between them. "Well, you're wrong. I've learned my lesson where you're concerned. I'll eat dinner with your family. I'll sleep with you, but without so much as a good night kiss. In short, I'll behave exactly as most American husbands do who are disillusioned with their wives."

He turned and strode into the bathroom, slamming the door behind him. Water splashed in the shower. A towel was ripped from a rack. She couldn't help but remember that first morning when they'd showered together, when he'd sweetly made love to her, pressing her against icy tiles while warm water rained over their bodies.

So much for marriage.

Never had she felt so rejected and hurt and alone.

Not that he was any happier. Not soon would she forget his ravaged face and dark, haunted eyes before he'd turned and left her.

What could she do about it? About any of it?

Josie leaned forward in her bed, her covers pulled up to her throat. Despite her best intentions not to worry about Adam, dread and anticipation caused her to start at every faint click of her brother's pool sticks, at every deep burst of Adam's laughter, at every raucous male shout that intermittently bubbled up from the billiard room.

The more cognac or port, or whatever they were all drinking, the more Adam roared with amusement, the more her brothers roared. Would he never tire of her brothers and come up to bed?

He did not want to come to her.

How could that hurt so much? When she'd repeatedly told him she didn't really want his big warm body lying next to hers? But she'd only said that because he'd married her out of duty and considered himself a disillusioned husband.

Why couldn't she just go to sleep and get this endless night over? Why couldn't she be happy he wasn't here? Why did she feel so agitated because he was down there having so much fun? Why did she feel so jealous and out of sorts because he fit in with her family and preferred them?

Brianna and her mother had been her only friends here. But Brianna had grown up, and her mother had long since retired to a fish camp on the bayou.

Why couldn't Josie just be glad she finally had a little time to herself? Dinner with Adam beside her, with her family's incessant, prying, faintly critical questions, had seemed interminable.

"Did you notice coming in how depressing New Orleans still is? I mean after the storms?" Marie Claire, Pierre's pretty blond wife, had said.

"Hurricanes, we call them, darling," Pierre said indulgently.

"The airport is still so depressing, don't you think, dear?" Gigi said. "I hope you told him it used to feel as diverse as our city was—full of all sorts of lively people rushing about and rich with the scents of beignets, Creole coffee and Cajun spices."

Josie hadn't admitted she'd been sulking when they'd landed.

"Our plane got in so late it was too dark to see much," Adam said, covering for her.

"The devastation goes for miles. We here in the Garden District are most fortunate," Gigi said.

Armand raised a fork. "Adam, you can't imagine how surprised I was when you called."

"Thrilled," Gigi said. "And then when we met you… Simply thrilled! I don't think any of us ever imagined Josie would bring home someone like you. Not after Banar—"

"Mother!" This from a desperate Josie.

"I was simply complimenting your new husband, dear."

"While criticizing me."

When Josie squirmed and tapped her foot on the Aubusson carpet, Adam's big hand covered hers and held on tightly.

"I'm sure I was just trying to indicate a polite, motherly interest in your Adam. I simply can't wait to brag to Sally and the rest of my Friday lunch group about my new son-in-law. A Ryder… Why the Ryders were real Texas pioneers. They hacked out a huge ranching, oil and gas empire from a tough land. They fought Indians and bandits and Union soldiers."

Josie felt hot color rising in her cheeks.

Pierre leaned forward. "How did you two meet, if you don't mind me asking? Are you into contemporary art, Adam?"

Josie flushed. Her brothers had met their gorgeous, blond wives socially. No way could she tell them she'd flaunted herself from her window while he'd watched from the dark.

Adam's voice broke in to her thoughts. "I'm afraid solid blobs of purple don't do much for me. Nor do giant rectangles painted solid black or white."

Everybody except Josie, who felt put down, laughed. When she tensed, Adam's finger, resting atop hers, began making soothing little circles.

"Back to how we met…"

His words, or was it his touch, sent a shock wave of alarm through Josie.

"I booked a room in her building. I saw her across the courtyard. In her window. I thought she was beautiful. Later we ran in to each other downstairs, and I thought she was even more beautiful."

Had he?

"I was starving and she was freezing, so I asked her to have dinner at a bistro. Then I was a perfect klutz and choked on a snail."

"I made him try it," Josie said.

"Josie does adore her escargots," Armand said.

"She was very fast on feet. Literally, she saved my life. When I opened my eyes, I found myself on the floor of that bistro, surrounded by surly French waiters. Not that any of that mattered to me in the least when I looked up and saw your beautiful daughter, hovering over me like my guardian angel."

"It must be an 'opposites attract' thing," Elise, who was Armand's exquisite blond wife, whispered breathily.

"Can we please—*please*—talk about something else?" Josie asked. "Hurricanes, maybe? Or blobs and squares of color that don't matter to anyone else except me."

"Why don't I tell everybody about Texas and my family," Adam began easily.

When her family encouraged him, he told them that from birth he'd grown up viewing the hard, sunburned faces of his ancestors on the ranch house walls. His father had preached that these brave pioneers had let nothing stand in their way, least of all their own weaknesses.

Adam told them that his father and grandfather had flown him over huge pastures, telling him the ranch would someday be his and that it was his duty to protect his family and the land.

He described his dominating father and his powerful, cultured mother, a complex woman who was closer to him than to anyone else now that his father was dead. He said they'd made incalculable demands on him and his brothers when they'd been boys, pitting them against each other and against every ranch hand. To toughen them, his father had claimed. Then Adam talked of the early days of the ranch.

When his audience warmed to his stories, his Wild West tales involving his ancestors grew livelier, and everyone, even Josie, whose hand he still held, listened spellbound until finally he brought her fingers to her lips in a false gesture of affection that made her mother smile and suggested that she might be tired.

His eyes had been so warm and kind, she'd thought he'd come up right after she had.

Hours later when the door finally opened, she went rigid. Listening to his heavy tread on the carpet and the whisper of his clothes as he shed them, it never occurred to her to think he might have stayed downstairs out of consideration for her. That he might have deliberately given her time to prepare for bed and fall asleep, so that she wouldn't have to endure his presence beside her in bed while she was conscious.

When he stood silently by the bed for a long time, she began to feel as if she might burst from the suspense. Was he never coming to bed?

"Adam?"

"You're awake?" His voice was low and rough.

"Couldn't sleep." She yawned. "I don't travel all that well."

"That I can understand."

Her covers slid off as she sat up. Too excited to care, she fumbled for the chain of the lamp beside her bed. "D-do you want me to turn on the light?"

"No...I'm not wearing much."

Neither was she. She yanked the beaded chain anyway. "I won't look then."

She covered her eyes but not before she'd seen him in his navy boxers. One glimpse of his virile, bronzed muscular torso feathered with dark hair sent fiery sparks sizzling through her.

Every part of him was lean and hard. His hands that hung at his sides were curled into fists.

His eyes were on her breasts, which were too clearly revealed by the golden lamplight slanting across her. Her night-gown was transparent, so he probably had no trouble making out the dark circles of her aureoles and her peaked nipples.

She shouldn't like his staring so much. She should lift the blankets and cover herself. Instead, the girl who'd stood in that window spoke huskily, invitingly. "Come to bed."

Abruptly, he turned his back to her. The mattress dipped, and she shut off the light. When he pulled back the sheets and slid in beside her he was careful not to tug the covers off her or touch her leg or arm. Still, it wasn't long before she felt the pleasant warmth of his long, muscular body invading her space beneath their shared blanket.

"Good night," she whispered, longingly, hoping for more.

When he didn't answer, she lay in the dark listening to the steady, harsh rhythm of his breathing. Could any man look at his wife as he just had and then fall asleep instantly?

Or was her "disillusioned" husband only pretending to ignore her?

"Adam?"

"I thought you wanted me to leave you the hell alone," he growled so viciously she was sure he hated her.

"I do," she lied, going rigid.

"Then do us both a favor and leave me the hell alone."

Fourteen

Separate beds, she'd said. No sex.

Adam lay in the dark, his muscles and nerves too tightly wound for sleep as he listened to Josie's even, shallow breaths and breathed in her sweet, floral scent. The instant she'd fallen asleep, she'd scooted across the bed and cuddled against him.

He'd drunk way too much booze playing pool to have complete control over his body. At her first touch, he'd become hotly aroused.

He'd known the danger. He should have pushed her away. Instead, he'd slipped his arm beneath her head. She'd whispered his name and snuggled closer, flinging a hand carelessly over his chest even as her boneless legs had tangled with his.

She felt too damn good. To hold her warm body like this with her silky hair tickling his throat and nose made him ache for her, burn for her.

Hell. She was putting him in hell. Not that he didn't deserve it.

When Josie moaned drowsily, Adam's eyes opened, and he stared up at the dark ceiling.

She didn't want him. He was probably violating her to be holding her like this. When she stroked him in her sleep, more fire shot through him, and his heart thudded unevenly.

If he wasn't careful, this would end as badly as his first marriage had. No matter what her motives were, the last thing he wanted was to derail her life or hurt her.

When she cried out in broken, panicked whispers against his ear, he tensed. Then she sighed and pressed her body even closer, so close it was all he could do to resist kissing her hard on the lips, to resist ripping her nightgown off and rolling on top of her.

Would she resist? Or kiss him back and spread her legs? Just the thought of her surrendering to him again drove him wild. So wild, he swore softly.

What the hell kind of relationship did they have anyway? She'd lured him from her window, and he'd jumped at her bait.

They'd had sex. Great sex. Incredible.

For weeks all he'd thought about was how she'd felt underneath him and then in the shower, her mouth and tongue making wild, wicked love just to please him. Even in Texas she'd haunted him. He'd avoided the hell out Abigail, refusing to even discuss Paris. He'd worked out in his gym twice as much. Even there when he'd been running so hard he'd thought his heart would burst, he'd hungered to have Josie's quivering body beneath his again, to feel her soft, sweet mouth open to his, to plunge deeply inside her again and again until finally he exploded in a blaze of glory.

Ever since he'd met her, he'd felt like a starving man.

Not that he meant much to her. When she'd found out who he was, she'd jumped at the chance to be rid of him. Would she have ever told him she was pregnant?

Even so, he wanted to protect her and the baby. To take care of her. But he didn't want to love her or to have her love him. He'd been unlucky in love as they say, but not nearly as unlucky as those who'd loved him.

Josie stirred, and he felt her lips against his shoulder again. The light caress of her warm lips and her soft hands running over his body made him go even crazier. He was burning up with desire.

She let out one of those soft little purrs and pressed her mouth to his shoulder again.

Damn. He wanted her more…way more than he had the night when she'd stood in her window.

Because now he knew how good she was.

Was she trying to kill him?

"Adam…. Adam…."

He clenched his hands.

Somehow he had to survive the night.

Like so many nights when she'd been an insecure teenager in this same bed, Josie was back in the swamp, alone on the Menards' barge.

Instead of familiar city sounds of traffic, sirens or dogs barking, she heard the wind in the swaying moss and the lapping of the water against the rusting sides of the barge. When an alligator slapped his tail, she jumped.

At some point her dream became a nightmare. She was slogging through the dirty water, her bare feet sinking deeply into the mud as snakes and alligators slithered after her. As always, she couldn't swim. When she crawled to the bank, branches cracked and tore behind her as the white alligators raced after her.

She had to run before their jaws snapped shut and they tore her to pieces. But she couldn't run.

Josie screamed and grabbed Adam. When he tried to push her away, she clung.

"Adam?"

He yanked the tangle of covers off her and cradled her against him.

"I—I was back in the swamp. They were going to eat me!"

His lips brushed her forehead. "Go back to sleep."

"As if…I could." Blindly she held on to him. "Hold me. Just hold me."

Slowly, gently, he rolled over and smoothed her hair off her damp brow.

"I was so lonely up here. I thought you'd never come to bed." She put her hands around his neck and muscular shoulders, pulling him down. Burying her face against his wide chest, she sobbed, holding on to him with all her strength.

"Josie, you've been crawling all over me all night. A man can stand only so much." There was a warning note in his husky voice.

"The alligators were big and white. When I was a little girl, they chased me up on the bank. Somehow I climbed on a low-lying branch, only I couldn't climb all that high because there was a brown snake in the tree and I didn't know if it was poisonous. So I stayed on the branch for what seemed like hours…until Daddy, only he wasn't my daddy really, until Mr. Menard got back in his pirogue from fishing."

"He left you alone."

"Not alone. Mama Menard was inside drunk, too drunk to hear my screams."

"God." Adam drew a shaky hand through her hair. Then he played with a loose tendril and brushed her cheek with the pad of his thumb.

"Daddy Menard was very angry when he saw me in that tree. He whipped me with his belt, yelling that he'd told me to stay on the barge."

Very gently Adam stroked her back and hair. "You're safe now."

"Oh, Adam," she sighed.

He said nothing, but after a minute or so, he pulled back from her a few inches.

She didn't want to let go of him—not ever, not when it felt so good to be held and comforted like this. All her life she'd craved such closeness. Never once had her mother or anyone else ever comforted her after a nightmare.

She closed her eyes, laid her head against his shoulder and simply held on to him until he began to rock her.

Guided by some instinct to prolong this special time, she stroked his hair, curling the thick, silky stuff around her fingertip. Then she spread her hands wide and ran them down over his chest.

His skin felt hot and moist, so hot her body began to blaze with new needs. Suddenly she was quivering all over. It was as if all her life she'd been waiting for him and this dazzling explosion of emotion that he'd evoked from that first instant when she'd sensed him in the dark.

Why him?

Why not him?

"Kiss me," she whispered.

When he stiffened, she opened her mouth and kissed his throat with her tongue.

"Josie, you did say no sex…."

"Did I?" She laughed. "A smart guy shouldn't remind a girl of stupid things she says, now should he?"

"But…I want to make you happy."

"Then hush." Her mouth moved along his rough jawline, exploring, tasting him, nibbling until she found his lips, which were open. "Make me happy."

He inhaled harshly.

"So you're not immune to me."

When her mouth met his in a searing kiss, his tongue danced inside her lips. One taste, and she sensed he wanted her as much as she wanted him. With more confidence, her hands moved down his body to the elastic waistband of his boxers, which she grabbed and tried to slide down his hips.

"Hey, what are you doing now?" he growled.

"Just this." Her hand closed over his erection. "And this." She squeezed him and began to stroke, slowly at first.

"I'm begging you," she whispered. "Please…please…make love to me."

Pulling away, he ripped his boxers off. When she realized he wasn't leaving her, she yanked her nightgown over her head and flung it after his shorts.

With a smile he lay back. Dark eyes glittering, his black head sank deeply into her pillows.

Slowly, her gaze locking on his, she crawled on top of him. Spreading her legs, she eased herself down, down, rubbing herself back and forth against him until he grabbed her buttocks and arched upward. With a wild, out-of-control cry, he drove into her.

For a long moment, he was still as he kissed her mouth and whispered love words into her ear. Then he plunged again and again, and with each thrust, she felt the walls around her heart and soul melting, until nothing separated her from him. Not her insecurity. Not her fear. Nothing.

When he shuddered, she exploded, weeping, laughing, sighing, and in that timeless moment, they were one.

Afterward, hungrily, greedily, she kissed any part of him her lips could reach—his eyelids, the tip of his nose, his mouth, his jaw, even his wide shoulders. Last of all she kissed his fingers, tasting them one by one.

Too aware of his tantalizing thickness still inside her, she brought his hand to her lips and traced the shape of each blunt finger with her tongue.

When she sucked a finger all the way inside her mouth, he pulled her head down and kissed her hard.

When finally he let her go, she smiled dreamily down at him. She felt strange and new and tender, like a baby or someone reborn.

A rush of sweetness washed over her. "Adam, oh, Adam, darling, my love…."

He frowned. When at last he tried to pull free, she clung.

"No, again… Do it again," she pleaded, kissing the center of his furred chest.

"Wanton!" He laughed and kissed her throat and then her lips.

She kissed him back, feeling as if he'd taken her to a new universe.

Sheets rustled, and he rolled off her, leaving her all alone. Wrapping himself in a quilt from the end of the bed, he opened the shutters and then the doors and went outside, trailing the quilt behind him. Leaning over the balustrade, he stood on the veranda in the soft, silvery darkness and stared out into the humid night.

"Adam?"

He didn't answer, and she felt the walls coming up between them again.

"What's wrong?" she whispered, feeling uncertain as she realized again how little she knew about him.

"Go back to sleep, my love. We'll talk in the morning." His tone was low and absent, his passion spent.

My love. Had that only been an idle endearment? Or did he mean it…a little?

She wanted to beg him to come back to bed. Instead, she sank back against the pillows, feeling empty and lost. If only he could love her someday…just a little. Maybe that would be enough.

She yawned and slid lower in the bed. Before she knew it she was asleep, so she never realized Adam didn't return to bed.

Fifteen

Josie was smiling even before she awoke to the soft beauty of an opalescent dawn flooding her bedroom. The scent of warm, buttery biscuits and frying bacon drifted up the stairway.

When she saw Adam's rumpled pillow, she reached for it, crushing it against her nose and gulping in his scent.

She felt wonderful this morning, maybe because last night had felt so perfect.

Where was he? Downstairs having breakfast with her brothers? Playing the perfect bridegroom and in-law again?

No longer was she angry at him for forcing her to come here or for working so hard to impress her family. Now she thought his efforts to make them proud of her sweet.

Ravenous hunger finally made her get up and pull on the first clothes she found, which, unfortunately, were her jeans. So anxious was she to see Adam, she forgot to comb her hair before flying downstairs.

No sooner had her toe touched the bottom stair, than Adam heard and rushed out of the dining room. When she saw him, she felt incredibly happy and yet shy, too.

He stopped in midstride, his black eyes so cold and dark, she sagged against the banister.

"Good morning, *my love*." A tense undercurrent in his tone made her heart beat at a frightening pace.

"What's wrong?" she whispered.

"I'm sorry about last night. I'm afraid I drank too much playing pool…with your brothers. If I offended you…I apologize."

"N-no. You didn't offend…." Her hand went to her throat. She tried to say more, to tell him she'd loved last night, reveled in it, but she couldn't.

All she could do was stare at him, feeling hopelessly lost and abandoned all over again. Would she always be the pregnant wife he'd had to marry?

"I'm sorry." His face was dark and stern. "It won't happen again. I swear it."

On the drive from the airport, Bob had done most of the talking. Josie hoped that Bob didn't notice the charged silence in the backseat of Adam's long black Mercedes that greeted all his remarks. Ever since that bleak moment on the stairs in New Orleans, Adam and she had barely spoken. Josie felt so shattered, she was barely able to function.

"Sir, I was sworn to secrecy by your mother, but I think I should warn—"

This from Bob in the front seat again as they sped up

Congress Avenue toward the domed capitol building on their way to Adam's home in west Austin.

Adam leaned forward, his dark face growing darker, probably because he hated bringing her home as his bride. "Out with it!"

"She's arranged a last-minute homecoming party for you."

"Damn."

Josie clenched the armrest and sent bangles jingling.

"It better be small and informal," Adam began. "And not one of her Texas-sized—"

"Sir, in her defense, I imagine she's so excited to hear the news of your marriage—"

"Not likely," Adam said as Bob braked in front of a pair of wide, chrome gates emblazoned with a pair of swirling, oversized *R*s.

Adam had told her his mother had sent him to Paris to convince her to stop dating Lucas. Why would she allow such a party?

No sooner did the impressive gate with the huge Ryder brand swing open, than Adam's modern, hand-cleaved, lime-stone mansion and the enormous white party-tent set up on the lawn loomed before them.

Josie gasped. "Your house is gorgeous."

Dozens of luxury cars gleamed in the sunlight. Valets in white shirts raced about.

"I—I should have changed," she said as someone cut a thousand red balloons loose and they began drifting upward into a clear, blue sky. The glittering throng under the tent yelled before stomping en masse to greet the Mercedes.

"Where'd she find all these damn people—" Adam cursed under his breath.

"For what it's worth, I tried to talk *them* out of it."

"*Them?*"

"Your mother. Abigail."

"Abigail, too?" Josie tensed.

The tall, older woman with the youthful, long-legged stride at the head of the glamorous crowd had to be Marion Ryder. Like Adam, she was deeply tanned, and her short hair was streaked with silver. Circling her, a pair of frenzied Scottish terriers bounced up and down, their black tails waving as they yapped.

Marion threw her arms around Adam. Both terriers bolted into the Mercedes and began to paw Josie, their wet noses sniffing her denim jeans. When Bob yelled at them to stop, they laid identical black chins on her knees and stared up at her with apologetic brown eyes.

"Meet my dogs, Lucy and Jack," Bob said. "They've failed obedience school more times than I care to admit. Mainly they stay out back with me, but they love parties, food and meeting new people."

At the sound of their names, Lucy and Jack looked at Bob and whined, but when Bob turned around, they nudged their noses even higher up Josie's thigh.

Finally Marion let go of Adam, so he could turn and collect Josie. Although nerves had given Josie a headache and a stomachache, she forced a smile.

Adam snapped his fingers and said something that sent the terriers scrambling out of the car. Nails scraping on the drive, they flew around the back of the house.

Relieved, Josie stood up, to be introduced to Marion.

Adam's mother regarded her critically for a long moment before taking her hand, which she pressed lightly and quickly released.

"Welcome to Austin," she said in a voice that lacked warmth even as she turned to smile at a darkly-gorgeous, slim, young woman in a black suit who'd positioned herself beside Adam as if she thought she belonged there. "Abigail, darling…."

Abigail smiled. "I'm an old friend of the family's. Of Adam's."

Aware of Adam's heightened color, Josie glanced down at her feet.

"We're all so excited to meet you. Since you didn't have a real wedding, Marion and I just had to do something…to introduce you to all of Adam's friends. Marion did the flowers. Aren't they wonderful?"

Marion looked everywhere except at Josie.

"Wonderful," Adam bit out.

Suddenly Josie longed for a bathroom where she could bathe her face with cold towels. She felt flushed and tired and incapable of dealing with the more poised Abigail and the conflicted Marion.

Adam put his hand on Josie's elbow, and her bangles jingled as he led her toward the house. They got as far as the front stairs before they were mobbed again.

With his arm draped around her waist, he introduced her to his partners, neighbors and friends. The last person to shake her hand was a woman with fierce brown eyes, a firm jaw, and thick glasses. She wore a plain brown suit that had probably been in her closet for years.

"Camille Vanderford."

"My secretary," Adam said.

Camille regarded Adam sternly even as she continued to hold on to Josie's fingers. "You, my dear, have your work cut out for you. I should know."

Adam grinned.

"Don't hesitate to call me if he and his mother don't behave themselves. I'll straighten them out for you."

Josie laughed. "Even his mother?"

"Marion and I go back a long way."

Finally, after she'd met everyone, Adam led her inside.

Although immense, the house was sleek and simple with shiny wooden floors, stone walls and high ceilings. Everything seemed to be white or gray. Other than the large bouquets Marion had set on every flat surface, there was no color and absolutely no art on the walls.

Boring. Maybe he needed her, after all.

It was strange, how his magnificent house didn't reflect Adam in any way. It was as if the architect had vanished, and the owner had never moved in.

Adam led her to a bathroom that was filled with pink roses and daisies, where she washed her pale face and applied fresh lipstick that seemed too bright. Not liking the way she looked, she sat down on a low bench and tried to summon the strength to face Adam's friends, especially the lovely Abigail. Maybe she would have stayed there forever, had Adam not knocked on the door and called her name.

"People are asking for you," he said, peeping in at her. "You're the guest of honor."

She nodded and let him take her arm and lead her out to the terraces, where a live band played and vocalists sang.

The day was crisp and springlike. People were friendly, and she began to enjoy herself. The party went on and on. The food and entertainment were too wonderful for anybody to want to leave.

Adam stayed at her side for hours as the partygoers drifted about the yard, talking, laughing, eating and enjoying themselves immensely. When he finally left her, his friends came up one at a time to share their cute stories about Adam.

She was fine for a while, but when Adam didn't return she grew so tired, she escaped into the house. She was rushing through the immense living room with its high white walls and sheets of glass when his mother joined her with glasses of champagne.

"The house was built here for the views of oaks, limestone cliffs and cedar," Marion said, sipping her champagne while Josie twirled hers. "You're close to downtown, but you feel almost like you're in the country."

Too tired to think of anything to say, Josie nodded.

"So you were a friend of Lucas's?" Marion frowned thoughtfully.

"Lucas and I met at a Picasso exhibit. We were friends."

"Really?"

"Really."

A beat passed. "So, you're an artist?"

"I try."

"Unlike Lucas, Adam has never been one for the arts."

Josie didn't know what to say to that, so she held on to her champagne and stared at the empty white walls that cried out for adornment.

"We were all so surprised when Adam called and said he'd married you."

"Shocked, I imagine."

"Yes."

"I'm sorry things had to be such a surprise and so rushed," Josie said. "He probably can't believe it's happened himself. I know I—"

"He was very young when he married the first time. He's always shown immense resistance to the idea of marrying again—until you. Has he ever told you about Celia?"

What was she driving at? "He told me about Abigail." Josie began twisting her flute stem around and around.

"Oh, dear, I'm saying all the wrong things."

Was she? "I know the feeling." Josie swirled the champagne in her glass so rapidly she splashed some on the floor. "Sorry."

"Oh, dear, I—I've been terrible. I hope I haven't offended you."

"No, it's hard to make small talk sometimes, hard for anybody…when you don't know a person well or when you've had a shock like this."

Josie bit her bottom lip and watched the swirling gold liquid in her flute make bubbles. "Well, he didn't exactly have a choice, did he?"

"What? What are you saying?"

"He *had* to marry me."

"Oh? Again? Oh!" Marion's gaze swept Josie's untouched flute of champagne, her pale face, her full breasts and her flat stomach with the fascination of a longtime animal breeder. "I see," she said a long time later. Marion sighed. "Then I wouldn't push him to tell you about Celia. Wait until he's ready. He can't forgive himself for what happened, you see."

"I don't understand."

"He's a good man. Too good for his own good, sometimes. He means well by this I'm sure."

Was she saying he shouldn't have married again? Josie felt wretchedly confused.

"He'll be good to you—if you let him," Marion said.

Josie expected criticism and censure. To her surprise, Marion's narrow, angular face softened. "Well, this isn't all bull," she whispered, "maybe *this time* I'm really to be a grandmother. We've suffered…this family… Adam especially… We need a baby. He needs a baby. Maybe this time… Yes! We must make the best of this!"

In the next moment, she set Josie's champagne down and then took Josie by the arm. "I'll get you some water. You look absolutely parched. And exhausted. Come. There's a chair over there in the corner. Adam should have told me everything. Then I never would have had this party. We must get rid of all these people so you can rest."

All her life Josie had wished to be mothered. Gratefully, she followed Marion to a large, overstuffed chair near a tall window.

"This is Adam's favorite place to read. It has the best view of all and wonderful light."

Beyond the dark fringe of a hilltop, the capitol's dome could be seen. With a grateful sigh, Josie sank into the deep softness of the chair.

She relaxed, sipping water in Adam's wonderful chair until she felt the need to find a bathroom again. Then she arose and wandered down a hall, opening doors.

The third door revealed a shadowy room with tall ceilings and high walls lined with leather books. When she heard Adam's deep voice mingle with Abigail's softer tones, she froze.

"I understand…. I'll wait…until this whole dreadful thing is over," Abigail said.

Josie stumbled backward into the hall.

"No," Adam said.

When the door banged lightly against the wall, Josie jumped. Why hadn't she been more careful? Embarrassed, she ran down the hall, opening every door until at last she slipped into a large bathroom that bloomed with yellow tulips and red roses.

She grabbed a towel and wet it. With shaking hands, she pressed a cool cloth against her face. Her eyes were closed, and her head ached when the door opened and shut.

"Josie," Adam began.

She jumped at his deep, distressed voice. "You don't have to leave her and come after me or pretend you care…."

He cursed quietly. "Dealing with Abigail…and my mother…this party… Surely you understand that this is the last thing I wanted today."

"Like our marriage?" Her mouth felt as dry as dust.

"What?"

"You heard me," she said.

"And last night? Was that the last thing you wanted?" His voice was rough.

"Maybe…yes…yes!"

"Damn you. Then why the hell did you say you wanted me?"

"It meant nothing," she lied, pressing her hot face deeper into the cold cloth. She wasn't about to admit the truth after catching him with Abigail. "It was just sex. Nervousness. Bridal jitters. I was scared and lonely. You were there. You know how little sex means…to a woman like me. I'm not as saintly as…your precious Abigail."

"Is that the truth?" He ripped the cloth from her hands and flung it down onto the marble floor. When she would have run from him, he grabbed her wrists and yanked her against his body, so that she felt his heat and the heavy beat of his pounding blood.

"I guess I was in the mood," she whispered even as her body prickled in sensual awareness of him.

He tilted her chin so that he could study her face. He swallowed. She could feel his hands shaking. He was violently upset.

"You're pale," he muttered. "You're trembling. Why?"

"Because you grabbed me! Because you're scaring me!"

Josie shut her eyes, hoping, praying he couldn't see how deeply he'd hurt her.

"Last night it wouldn't have mattered who you were," she lied.

"I could have been any stranger...in a window? Lucas—would he have been even better?"

How could he think that?

Beneath his furious gaze, she felt sick with humiliation. But when she didn't deny it, he sucked in an angry breath and pushed her from him.

"All right. I understand. This is a business deal to you—pure and simple. Don't crawl all over me and beg for it again, understand?"

"Yes." Her low voice was raw, tortured.

He spun on his heel, and she caught a final glimpse of his dark, enraged face in the mirror.

Good. She'd made him as miserable as she was.

Feeling shattered and exhausted, she sagged against the wall. Long minutes later when she stumbled out of the bathroom and nearly into him, she was anything but composed.

"What are you still doing here?" she shrieked, jumping back.

"Waiting for you. We're married, remember? We're in love."

At the sight of Adam looking as lost and unhappy as she was, a shock of utter misery went through her. Why had she married him?

He nodded curtly, and she followed him down the hall into the living room, where his mother, who looked almost light-hearted, and several guests lingered by the windows.

His mother left the others and came up to them, smiling at Josie. "Adam, she told me about the baby! I'm so thrilled."

A wash of color scalded Adam's face. Not that he answered his mother by look or word.

"Did Adam tell you, he's convinced Lucas to give up his novel and take a teaching job here in Austin?"

"But, Adam, Lucas's writing means so much to him," Josie cried.

Someone called to Marion, and she excused herself.

"Why would you make him give up his writing?" Josie persisted.

"Maybe it's time he grew the hell up."

"Do you blame him…for what happened…? For the baby…for our marriage?"

"Hell no."

"You're punishing him, aren't you?"

"You should be happy. Next time you're in the mood he'll be close by." Adam hurled himself away from her.

"But I want you," she whispered in a strangled tone to an empty room. "Only you."

The windows were open, and cool breezes flowed into the kitchen when Josie tiptoed downstairs the next morning. Someone, probably Bob, had made coffee and set out boxes of cereal and a skillet and butter.

When she wandered out of the kitchen into the living room and dining room, all was in perfect order. Bob must have stayed up late to clean up after the party.

She returned to the kitchen and poured herself a cup of coffee. Birds were twittering in the oaks, and squirrels were racing up the pecan trees outside. Last night right before she'd fallen asleep, she'd heard two owls hooting to each other from a high branch beside her bedroom. She could be happy here if only…

But where was Adam? She hadn't seen him since they'd

quarreled about Lucas. He'd sent Bob to show her to her room. Had he already left for work? Without saying goodbye? Was he deliberately avoiding her as he'd promised?

Adam had had most of her possessions packed and sent ahead. Suddenly she wondered if they'd arrived yet. If they hadn't, what would she do with herself all day alone in Adam's huge, immaculate house?

She found eggs and fresh fruit and milk in the refrigerator. Deciding not to cook, she made herself a bowl of cereal with strawberries.

After breakfast, despite Adam's warnings about Bob's territorial instincts, she washed her dishes before sitting down to read the Austin newspaper.

When she was finished with it, she was so restless she called Brianna.

"So, how's married life?" Brianna asked.

"Fine."

"That's what you say…when things aren't so fine."

"Look, I called because it would be great if you'd let me know if you see anything interesting, I mean a job, say in nine months…."

"For you? But why?"

"Don't tell anybody, but Adam is going to divorce me then."

"What?"

The hairs on the back of Josie's neck prickled. Then she heard a footstep behind her.

Turning, she nearly jumped out of her skin when she saw Adam striding into the kitchen. He wore a dark suit and carried a bulging briefcase.

"I—I thought you'd already gone to work," she whispered.

"Obviously."

Remembering their quarrel, Josie felt uneasy and yet hurt and shy, too.

How much had he heard? Did he even care that she was already looking for a job?

"We did say we'd tell no one our marriage isn't real for the time being."

"Brianna doesn't live here."

"I need to talk to you. Tell her you'll call her back."

Josie whispered a hurried goodbye while Adam poured himself a cup of coffee. When she hung up, he turned.

"I made an appointment for you at four this afternoon," he said. "With Dr. Moore, a leading obstetrician."

"Without even asking me?"

He ignored that. "Moore's the best. It was damned hard to get the appointment. I'm flying to Houston this afternoon. Research for a client. So Bob will have to drive you to Dr. Moore's. I thought you'd be glad to have something to do since your things won't be here until tomorrow."

"Oh." Suddenly she felt like apologizing and begging him to stay.

"I'll see you in six or seven days," he said.

"*A whole week?* But…don't you want to meet the doctor, too?"

Adam's black eyebrows lifted in surprise. "You'd actually want me there?"

Yes. She wanted him in town, period.

She tossed her head with what she hoped was an air of indifference. "You're right. Silly me. Hormones. I guess it doesn't matter."

In reality, she was acutely disappointed. The baby was the one thing they had in common, the one link that might bring them closer.

"Some other time then," he muttered, but he was watching her, and his tone was strange, almost edgy. He started to say something else and then stopped himself.

"What?" she whispered.

"Nothing important," he growled.

"Tell me," she pleaded.

"Later."

"But you're going away. You'll forget."

"Right."

She'd felt he'd softened by the time he set his cup down and blurted out an offhand goodbye, so she trailed him out to his car like a lost puppy and watched as he got in his sleek Mercedes. She even ran after his car as he backed down the drive.

He hadn't apologized or kissed her, but when he reached the gate, he waved and smiled.

That was something. Grinning and waving, she ran out the gate and stood there long after his Mercedes had disappeared.

Was Abigail going to Houston with him?

Sixteen

"Do you want to know the gender?"

"Oh, my God! *That's* really my baby?" Josie felt total awe. "Yes! Yes, to answer your question."

The baby's heart thumped loudly, or was it Josie's own heart making all the noise?

Josie couldn't stop listening to the heartbeat or staring at the black-and-white images on the monitor of her baby swimming about in her womb.

"It's a little boy," the young sonographer in purple scrubs said.

"I thought it would be too early to tell the sex?"

"It's early. Sometimes I can't tell nearly so early. But see—right here." She pointed at the screen. "You have to know what to look for, but I'm nearly sure it's a boy."

Someone knocked on the door. Then a nurse pushed it open and stepped inside. "Somebody's here to see you, Mrs. Ryder."

"Josie?"

Josie started at Adam's deep, apologetic voice.

"I hope I'm not too late," he said.

"Adam!" she squealed, smiling as soon as she saw his dark, worried face. "Adam? Oh, I'm so glad…you're here to see this. Look—our precious little son!"

"A son?" He stared at her and then at the screen. As he watched their little boy, his eyes filled with awe, and his expression softened.

He took her hand and pressed it to his lips.

"Can you make a print of that?" Adam whispered to the sonographer.

"Yes. And a DVD, too."

"Adam, she said I can probably feel the baby move around, that this early a lot of first-time mothers don't realize what they're feeling."

The sonographer slid the DVD and prints into a manila envelope.

Slowly, Josie pulled his hand toward her belly and then held it there. "Adam, I think he's moving! Yes! Yes! Can you feel it?"

He shook his head.

"It won't be long," the sonographer said.

"I'll drive you home when you're done seeing the doctor," Adam said.

"What about Bob? And Houston?"

"I sent Bob home to cook for you. As for Houston, I'm taking a later flight. I wouldn't have missed being here today with you for anything."

"Oh."

She grinned. On the way home, she sat up front beside him, and they happily discussed baby names like any married couple.

"Jacob's definitely my favorite," he said. "It was my father's name. My middle name, too."

"And I like Daniel."

She laid her head back against the rich dark leather headrest.

They were almost home when he said, "I guess I could live with Danny."

"Jacob Daniel," she whispered, turning shyly. "We could call him Jake."

"Jake," he repeated, and she thrilled to the tenderness in his low tone.

When Josie's things from Paris arrived in huge boxes the next morning, Bob hauled them on a dolly into a big room off the garage with lots of glass windows and skylights.

With Bob's help, she quickly began unpacking, but once she had her easels set up and had opened her paints, the smell of oil and turpentine was so strong she had to open all the windows.

Bob admired her canvasses, especially her gargoyles, saying he had a few monsters of his own. Then he left, and she walked back and forth, staring at her canvasses, trying to summon the willpower to paint. But the gargoyles didn't fascinate her nearly as much as they had in Paris. After seeing the doctor, she couldn't stop thinking about the baby. And in the end she went into the house to watch the DVD again.

After she finished, the baby moved. With her hand on her stomach, she climbed the stairs and wandered from bedroom to bedroom.

The bedroom between hers and Adam's was small and sunny. She loved its views of the trees and the downtown buildings and the yard. Running to the nearest house phone, she called Bob.

When he answered, Lucy and Jack were yapping so loudly, she could barely hear him.

"You've got to come upstairs."

"What?"

"Now. I need you to move the furniture out of the middle bedroom and store it."

"Shouldn't we ask Adam first?"

"Probably. But he isn't here, so I think I'll surprise him."

"He's not much on surprises."

"I want to create a nursery. A yellow nursery, I think. Can you paint?"

"You're going to paint the nursery yellow?"

"No, you are."

"Me?" Bob said.

"Adam said you were wonderful around the house. I'm not supposed to stand on ladders, you know."

"Do you swear I'll have a job…if we do this?"

"Hey, what's with your tattoos and motorcycles, if you don't like to live dangerously?"

It was only six in the afternoon. Still, Adam was exhausted from his three endless days and nights in Houston as he drove into his dark garage.

He'd cut his trip short because he hadn't been able to stop thinking of Josie's shy smile as she'd held his hand while they'd watched their son on the monitor together.

He got out of his car, grabbed his briefcase and overnight bag and raced into the house. For the first time ever, he hadn't stopped by the office on his way home from a trip.

As he unlocked the back door, he heard his brother laugh. Then Josie's laughter joined Lucas's.

A thick manuscript with Lucas's name on every page of it lay scattered across the kitchen table. Upstairs Josie said something low and husky, and Lucas laughed again.

A suffocating passion gripped Adam as he flung his briefcase and bag down on top of the manuscript and strode up the stairs and then down the hall to the middle bedroom. Without knocking he threw the door open.

"Adam?" Josie's breath caught. Then a slow grin spread across her face. Either she was the best damned actress in the world, or she really was overjoyed to see him.

Her eyes shining, she took a single step toward him before stopping.

Behind her his mother and Bob stood together in a newly bright, mustard-colored bedroom. Ten feet away, across from them, Lucas was balancing a pair of ridiculous-looking red circus clowns against the wall.

"What the hell?" Adam muttered.

The red clowns clattered onto the polished maple floor.

"You scared the hell out of me," Lucas grumbled. "You should have knocked."

"In my own damn house?"

"You were supposed to be gone a week," Josie whispered. "The nursery was going to be a surprise."

"Won't it be wonderful?" Marion said. "Josie's designed it all by herself. Bob painted it. Who would have thought of this beautiful yellow?"

"Well, it's certainly yellow," Adam said, blinking because the walls glowed like neon.

"It's the color of sunshine," Josie whispered.

She beamed with such pride and fearful happiness that he didn't dare tell her what he really thought.

"It's great," he said. "Sunshine, you say."

Bob expelled a long breath and visibly relaxed.

"Have you seen the DVD of your baby yet?" Marion asked.

"Not since I left for Houston."

"Well, I want to see it again before I go," Marion said. "Would you care to join me?"

What he wanted was to crush Josie into his arms. Instead, he led the way to the DVD player in his home theater, and sat with his mother and the group, and they all watched the DVD together.

When everyone finally left, Adam stole up behind Josie in the kitchen and placed a package wrapped in blue tissue on the counter.

"What's this?" she asked.

"Just open it."

She tore into the wrappings like a greedy child and then smiled as she pulled out a silver frame.

"It's for the sonogram of Jacob Daniel," he said.

Her eyes were luminous as she ran a shaking hand along the edges of the blue-jeweled frame. "Blue for our little Jake.... Why, thank you, Adam. Thank you so much! Already, he's beginning to seem...real."

His breath caught, thickened. Would she ever think anything about their forced marriage was real...besides their baby?

Suddenly, he ached to pull her into his arms. If only he could apologize for what he'd done in Paris.

Hell. Maybe it was enough that she was smiling at him for now.

"I'll hang those clowns for you," he said, not daring to touch her or say anything too personal for fear he'd scare her off.

Still smiling, she followed him into the mustard-colored nursery. When he finished hanging the clowns and set the hammer and extra nails down on the dresser, he stood beside her and they admired the red sculpture together.

"Can you believe the clowns were sitting in front of our neighbors' house to be thrown away?"

He could, but he knew better than to say so, so he shook his head.

"Well, I brought them to the studio and painted them."

He smiled. "It's nearly seven. You hungry?"

"Bob and I didn't know you were coming home, so I'm afraid there's not much for dinner in the house," she said.

"I've been wanting to try that new place right around the corner, where all the college kids sit at picnic tables and eat while they work on their laptops."

She nodded. He took her hand, and they walked along the shady, limestone path in the park to the café. Inside the restaurant she stood in line beside him while he ordered their sandwiches and soft drinks.

"And a pickle," she said. "I love pickles."

"Make that five pickles," he said to the cashier. "And maybe some sardines."

"We don't have sardines, sir."

Josie laughed.

Before long their order came, and they found a picnic table under a shady live oak out back. They talked easily about all sort of things for a while. She was munching the last of her fifth pickle, when he pushed his own food aside.

"I'd better tell you I had to get married the first time, too, before my mother does. Did she mention Celia?"

"She did, but she stopped herself."

"I should never have gotten involved with her, but I was young, in my second semester at Yale. My older brother had died the previous summer, and I couldn't get over it. My family expected me to be stoic, but I'm afraid I began to run pretty wild. Celia, who was part of that wild crowd, fell in love with me, so I slept with her. We were careless, and she got pregnant. Turned out she was a nice kid from a nice family. I wasn't ready for marriage. When she lost the baby, I divorced her, rather callously, I'm afraid. She loved me, truly loved me, and I hurt her so badly, she's never married or had children by anybody else."

"Neither have you."

"She made a lot of mistakes. Bad men…drugs. Her life's been a downward spiral. Her family blames me."

"And you do, too."

"I made her very unhappy. She deserved better than I gave her."

"And you haven't forgiven yourself, have you? Well, she made some bad choices. And I—I know what that's like. Not long ago…I—I met this man…an artist. I thought he loved me for myself. I opened up to him and told him things I resented about my family that I shouldn't have told him, about how my mother treated me. I didn't know that he was going to use everything I said to enhance his name and attack my family. The night I found out why he was dating me, he shot a final video of me. He even put that in this awful video sequence he did attacking my family. He exhibited it and me…both in a museum and on the Web. And because he did, I hurt myself and my family terribly. They had to pay him off to shut him up. Now I think all he ever intended was to use me to blackmail them." She reached out and stroked his hand. "So, I know what it's like to have regrets. To hurt people you care about."

Lightning flickered toward the western hills, and a little while later thunder rumbled.

Suddenly he felt exhausted, drained. He didn't like to think about her with Barnardo. Why the hell had he brought up Celia?

He stood up, and she stacked their plates while he gathered and threw away their garbage. When they'd cleaned up, he took her hand and she leveled her gaze at him.

He felt her compassion. More than anything he wanted to pull her close and kiss her hard. Instead, he inhaled a sharp breath and folded her fingers through his.

With a casual air, he led her deeper into the growing dark and was rewarded for his restraint when she talked easily of ordinary things. As the evening breezes gusted about them, he suddenly felt happy and vitally alive as they raced home beneath the trees.

No sooner, however, was he standing beside her at their front door, than new tensions filled him.

Blissfully unaware of his feelings, she put her hand on his waist and leaned forward. "I'm glad you came home early."

"Me, too."

He unlocked the door and opened it. He couldn't forget making love to her in New Orleans. He wanted to pull her close and kiss her, to carry her up the stairs and then strip her and make love to her as he had before.

Had he not lain awake for hours in his hotel room last night imagining her beneath him, imagining her soft body was his to stroke and kiss until she cried out for him to take her?

He wanted her legs wrapped tightly around him and her mouth on his shaft.

"Thank you…for the clowns…for supper…for everything," she said shyly.

Blindly he bent his head to nuzzle her soft red curls, and that was all it took for his pulse to begin beating too abruptly. His erection, which was already thick and hard, strained against his jeans. All he had to do was pull her close, and she would know how much he wanted her.

"I missed you…the whole time I was gone. I'm sorry we quarreled," he said.

The wind gusting from the park caught her hair and blew it against his cheek. She shivered.

"I missed you…a lot, too," she said, her voice and hand shaking as she clutched his sleeve.

"I couldn't stop thinking about how beautiful you were…in New Orleans."

"I—I should go up to bed," she whispered in a faltering tone as she skittered across the threshold. "You must be tired."

"Not really."

She didn't answer him. Instead, she flew up the stairs.

The last thing he heard when he stepped inside was the sound of her dead bolt as she locked him out.

Lightning burst against the black sky outside Josie's window. Not that she was thinking about the wild rain lashing the eaves or the wind that tore huge branches out of the pecan trees and flung them down so hard the whole house shuddered.

She wanted to open the windows and let the wind blow through the house. She wanted Adam to kiss her until she was breathless. She wanted him to carry her down the hall and ravish her.

For three days, she'd dreamed of him.

Suddenly another branch banged violently onto the roof above her bedroom, clattering as it rolled off. When it crashed down onto the drive, Adam's door opened. She sat up as when he padded heavily down the hall and then raced down the stairs.

The front door opened. Long minutes later, she heard it

close again. He remounted the stairs, only this time, his heavy footsteps stopped outside her door.

She threw off her covers and raced across her bedroom and pressed her ear to the wood. Did she only imagine that she heard the measured rasps of his breathing?

Finally, he got his breathing under control, and she heard his retreating footsteps down the hall. When his door opened, she unlocked her own and called his name.

"Adam?"

In the shadowy hall she could only dimly make out his dark, broad-shouldered body in pajama bottoms.

"Are you all right?" he said.

For a long moment she could barely breathe, much less speak. "I—I'm fine," she said at last.

"Go back to bed."

She closed her door behind her and stayed in the hall. Then she ran to him.

"Scared of the storm?"

She threw her arms around his neck and pressed her body into his. "Maybe. Or maybe I just want you to hold me."

She laid her head against the curling black hair of his bare chest. Instantly his male scent mingled with the heat and power of his body, and she became dizzy.

"Don't do this," he muttered.

When she pressed herself closer, every muscle in his body corded.

"Would any man do tonight?" he growled, winding his arms around her waist.

"I should never have said that."

"Lucas? Was that why you had him over here? If I hadn't come home early today, would you have invited him to stay?"

She bristled at his scornful tone. "No, you big idiot. I didn't want anybody but you…in New Orleans. I was angry and hurt when I said those things. Maybe because I felt awkward and unsure around your friends…after I saw you in the library with Abigail. Maybe I didn't think we had a real marriage."

"I paid real money to marry you. That's all *you* wanted."

"No!" Her lips skimmed the shadowy hollow of his cheek. "I only named that high price because I wanted you to think the worst of me."

He stood very still, as if breathing in her warmth. "Why would you want that? That doesn't make sense."

Softly, she leaned closer and kissed the sensitive spiral of his ear. "Does everything always have to make sense?" she whispered, her voice husky, dreamy. "I'm an artist. Being quirky goes with the territory."

She threaded her fingers into the rough silkiness of his hair and wound a single tendril around a fingertip. "Either you want me or you don't…."

Slowly she turned away and began to walk down the silvery hall toward her room.

He hesitated for a mere fraction of a second.

"Josie…"

Her breath faltered, but she kept walking.

Then he was running, and she was running from him. He caught her halfway down the hall and pulled her gently into his arms. She was laughing as currents of fire stirred deep within her heart. Then he lifted her and whirled her around and around, before lowering her and backing her against the wall.

"Josie…Josie. What are you trying to do to me?"

His black eyes glittered darkly as he loomed over her. His

hands were on either side of her face. He began to pant even before he crushed her against the wall.

"You think I'm bad and wild, don't you?" she whispered. "Even when I'm fat and pregnant. I wasn't good enough for Lucas...."

"You're not fat...or bad," he whispered.

"Shut up." Shivering, smiling, she stood on her tiptoes and slanted her mouth across his.

"Maybe I am bad, because even if this is only a temporary marriage, I want you. *Not Lucas.* You! I'm your wife. Why shouldn't I enjoy you, at least, as long as we're married?"

Her hands trembled as they slid up his chest and shoulders and then down his arms.

"Oh, God," he muttered.

She made some broken sound.

His answering kiss was long and desperate. His tongue thrust inside and explored her mouth. When he finally released her, she was shaking and gasping, dying for more.

His breath came swiftly as he stared into her eyes. Then with big, rough hands, he stroked the sides of her face and the length of her throat. On a shudder, his hands fell away, and he simply stared at her.

"Adam?"

"My precious darling, I can't believe..."

When she put her hands around his neck, he lifted her into his arms and carried her down the hall. Upon entering his room, he kicked the door shut behind him. Then he strode to his bed and laid her down.

He was easing himself down on top of her, when she put her hand against his warm, brown chest, pushing against him. "Not yet...."

"What? But I thought…"

"Not so fast," she murmured.

"What?"

"Stand up again, just for a second."

When he did so, she said, "Now, take off your clothes….
No…"

As she stared up at his tall, muscular body she felt a sensual
tightening deep inside her belly. "I want you to strip…but
slowly…while I lie here and watch. I like to watch, remember."

He unbuttoned his pajama bottoms and let them slide to the
floor.

Then he stood in the dark without moving while her wild,
green eyes devoured him.

Seventeen

Adam woke up with Josie's sweet, warm body wrapped around his. Heaven. She was heaven. Never in his whole life had he felt so happy. It was crazy. It wouldn't last. Still, lying beside her was pure bliss.

One glance at her beautiful, white neck and wildly tangled red hair reminded him of the rapture and wildness of the night before, of her body atop his, of her red tangles brushing his cheek and shoulders as she'd eaten him. She'd driven him up, up, over soaring edges.

Yawning, she sat up slowly and stretched. He tried to pull her closer, but she said in a soft, ethereal tone, "Just a sec. I have to get up and go to the bathroom. I'll be right back! Promise!"

She kissed his nose and rubbed her cheek against his. Then with a long sigh, she was gone.

Smiling, he lay back and cradled his hands beneath his head

as she padded softly to the bathroom. Pregnant ladies spent a lot of time in bathrooms, he'd learned.

He was still smiling as he listened to the morning doves when she gave a little cry and then began to scream and scream. He was in a state of shock before he rolled over and saw the blood…. Her blood…everywhere. In a daze he touched the red sheets, and his hands became wet and warm and sticky.

"Adam!"

He sprang out of bed, yelling her name, as he sprinted toward the bathroom.

She emerged quietly. Her face was ashen. Her huge, black pupils were dilated with fear.

"Adam…oh, Adam. It's everywhere. I can't stop it."

"Darling…"

He rushed to her and held her for a long moment, his unshaven face rasping against her soft, tear-streaked cheeks. He stroked her hair and pulled her into his arms.

"It'll be okay," he whispered.

"But what if it isn't?"

His heart was slamming against his rib cage. "We'll get through it…somehow."

"Adam…"

"Trust me."

Then he was ripping towels off the racks and out of the cabinets, and helping her dress. He grabbed his cell and called Bob, yelling for him to get the Mercedes out of the garage and to call 9-1-1.

Then they were in the backseat of the car, and he was talking to Dr. Moore on his cell as he cradled her pale face against his chest.

The ten-minute drive to the hospital during morning rush

hour felt like a lifetime. Luckily, Bob had nerves of steel and the hospital wasn't that far. Even so, adrenaline and terror pumped through Adam's bloodstream and made every inch seem like a mile.

As he gazed down at her, she seemed to grow paler by the minute. Her eyes were closed now, her lashes casting crescent-shaped shadows across her blue-veined skin.

When they got to the E.R. and the men in white had her strapped down onto a gurney, Adam looked back and saw that her blood was all over the backseat. All over him.

"Go in with her. I'll take care of it," Bob said.

It would probably take him days to clean the car, Adam thought. The white-coated men whisked Josie away to some emergency exam room. Then Adam was led to a waiting room with a muted television and magazines.

Feeling crazed, he began to pace. He'd blame himself forever.

His stomach knotted while his hands shook. He felt gutless, scared senseless. Whether she died or lived, he would love her forever. Why had he let himself forget that he always hurt those who loved him?

Suddenly a series of heart-numbing images from Ethan's death bombarded him. Again he felt the heat in the thick brush and the thorns tearing his clothes. Again he heard Ethan shout and then the sound of his machete and then the bees…everywhere…a furious, swarming cloud…all over them…. Stinging him everywhere…right before everything went black.

When he'd awakened in the hospital, he'd wanted Ethan.

"He's gone," his mother had said quietly.

When Adam had slashed into the tree where the bees had been and the bees had attacked them, Ethan had slugged Adam, knocking him out. Then Ethan had thrown himself over his brother's unconscious body so that the enraged bees had mostly bitten him. Ethan had suffered too many bites to live.

His brother's sacrifice had taken a big piece out of Adam. It had been years before Adam had been able to come to terms with what he owed his brother and how he could pay him back.

Finally, since there was nothing he could think to do to help Josie, Adam stopped pacing and sank down into a tattered sofa and watched the silent screen. Never had he felt so alone or helpless, not even when he'd been told Ethan was dead.

Just when he thought he couldn't stand being there another second, a doctor—not Dr. Moore, but a harried-looking Dr. Norris—appeared.

Dr. Norris was short and gray-faced. He wore blood-stained, green scrubs.

"Mr. Ryder, it looks like your wife's having a miscarriage."

"But will she be all right?"

"She'll be fine…in time."

"Can I see her?"

The doctor nodded.

"Give me a minute." Adam buried his head in his hands. As he remembered their wildness and their fierce need for each other last night, he could only blame himself.

"This is all my fault. Last night I—"

"She told me about last night. This would have happened anyway."

"I don't believe you."

When Adam got a grip on himself, the doctor led him to the exam room. The door was shut, but Adam could hear Josie's wild sobs inside the room.

Would she hate him?

When he finally knocked and went in, she was still lying on

a gurney. Except for the dark circles under her eyes, her face was chalky white; her red hair tangled. An attendant was rolling up blood-stained sheets and absorbent pads.

"It was awful," Josie whispered. "The exam, I mean… It hurt…so much…. Our baby… I killed our baby!"

"No!"

Adam rushed to her and put his arms around her and was gratified when she clung to him. Not that that had to mean anything.

"I came as soon as they'd let me in," he said. "I'm sorry," he said. "I'm so sorry."

"Me, too. At least you won't be saddled with me anymore…. You'll be free…to marry whomever you want to. Abigail…"

His heart turned to ice. Every cell in his being seemed to die. So, he'd lost not only a son, but her.

"You'll be free, too," he whispered in a low, dead tone.

She closed her eyes and slumped against the gurney.

The door opened and a female technician with a pretty, heart-shaped face and blue eyes that shone like an angel's said, "Mrs. Ryder. We need to do a sonogram."

"Why? The doctor already said our baby's dead."

"It's just a technicality to confirm his medical opinion."

Half an hour later, Josie lay on the exam table with her eyes closed, still sobbing quietly. Adam stood behind the sweet technician with the lovely, heart-shaped face as she busily twisted knobs.

With dull eyes, Adam stared at the screen of the sonogram monitor as he waited for it to come on so they'd have the final proof that their baby was dead. Then they could leave.

Final proof that their marriage was dead.

At last the screen came on, and a grainy picture of their

baby wavered. With a sense of incredible loss, he looked at his poor little dead son and then leaned down and kissed Josie's brow.

Please God, let her be all right.

For a second she opened her eyes and stared at him. And then past him.

She stopped crying. Her mouth began to tremble at the edges even before the sound of a steady, throbbing heartbeat filled the exam room.

"Look," the technician cried. "We have a good picture now. What? Well, would you just look at that!" Her voice was breathless and filled with awe.

Slowly Adam's agonized gaze rose slowly to the gray screen again. When he saw his son and saw him move and heard his tiny beating pulse, a heavy stone seemed to lift off him.

Suddenly he could breathe again. For a long moment, he simply stared at the image of his son and listened to that miraculous heart that wouldn't stop beating.

It was Adam's turn to sob.

Slowly he knelt and lifted Josie's icy, white hand to his lips, kissing it fervently, grateful for this second, miraculous chance. Then, holding those bloodless fingers fast against his rough cheek, he felt the warm flood of his tears flowing over her fingers.

"Our heroic little son is still alive," he whispered against her ear. "He's still alive."

Adam clenched the phone as he paced his office. Why the hell didn't Josie answer? Bob had just called him on his cell and told him Josie and his mother were home.

As the phone rang and rang, Adam's heart sped up. He didn't want to go to Houston today without telling her that Cromwell, the head of the firm, was down with a migraine and needed him to head an important meeting in Houston.

Adam had promised her he'd take her to an art gallery opening in the neighborhood tonight, very briefly, of course, because of her delicate condition. The artist was a neighbor. Now they'd have to cancel.

He wanted to talk to her, to hear her voice, to let her know that he didn't want to leave her even for a night.

His recorded message answered.

Hell. He hung up and punched Redial. As he waited, he remembered her ashen face when she'd come out of his bathroom seven days ago.

He gripped the phone even tighter. At least his mother was with her.

In the week since the crisis, Adam had stayed home to take care of Josie. For long hours he'd sat beside her bed reading legal documents, reading novels—even Lucas's manuscript— and reading her art books, too, but always he'd been ready to run for anything she'd needed. He'd fed her, bathed her, held her. At night he'd lain beside her, listening to her breathing and thanking God that she and the baby were still alive.

Two days ago, when Dr. Moore, who had confined her to bedrest, had okayed light activity, she'd pulled Adam close and said, "Now, you really must return to work."

"If you'll ask your mother to come for a few days."

She'd shaken her head. "You still don't understand about my mother."

"What if I ask my mother?"

Hesitating only briefly, she'd nodded. When he'd called his mother and described the situation, Marion had dropped everything and had driven to Austin.

When his recorded voice answered again, he slammed the phone down so hard Vanderford buzzed him.

"Do you need anything, sir?"

Just for my wife to answer the damn phone!

"No."

Where the hell was Josie? At nine o'clock, she'd wrapped her arms around him and had kissed him goodbye. She'd promised, put her hand on heart and had done lots of other cute stuff, too, that she'd be better about answering the phone than she'd been yesterday.

"All you have to do is answer once to beat that lousy record," he'd said.

"It's just that I think Bob and your mom are here, and your house is so big, and when it keeps ringing, I start running all over the place looking for the phones," she'd answered.

"Don't run," he'd ordered.

"I was trying to explain why I don't get to the phone."

"Carry one with you."

"I tried that, remember, and I lost two phones, which was why I missed the rest of your calls."

Was she the most disorganized woman in the whole world? He dialed her again, and the phone immediately went to voice mail.

God. Why did he think about her all the damn time? Why couldn't he forget that the first thing she'd said after she'd thought she'd miscarried was that he could leave her?

What would he have to do to make her understand he wanted her, not just the baby?

With her pregnancy so precarious, he couldn't woo her with kisses and sex now.

He ran his fingers through his hair. He'd better wrap his mind around his work for a change.

Adam stared at the piles of stacked documents on his desk—closing statements, deeds, memos, urgent messages from clients, Post-it notes with lists of more names to call. He had so many fires to put out, he didn't know where to begin.

His overnight bag stood beside his door so he could grab it on the run when Bob called him from the car. Well, he'd better do what he could before he had to go.

Adam buzzed Vanderford and told her to ring Josie and put her through the second she answered. Then he began throwing alphabetized files into his briefcase to read on the plane.

He was about to call Bob when the door opened, and Abigail slid inside. When he arose, she came around his desk and sat down in his chair as she used to when they'd dated.

"I was worried about you," she said. "You've seemed so distracted and unhappy...ever since Paris. And then, last week...when I heard about the baby."

Quickly he crossed the room and closed the door to Vanderford's outer office.

"I should have told you about Josie immediately."

Abigail got up and came around to him. She reached up and fingered his tie as she had in the past. Stunned, he took a step backward, but she quickly followed.

"Remember how it was between us before you left for Paris at Christmas? *We* were to be married."

"None of that matters now."

"I understand about the baby and even how it could have happened." Her voice was soft and charged and yet compassionate, too. "I mean, we both worked all the time. We were gone a lot, too. We'd been taking each other for granted for a long time. Adam, I swear, if you'll give me another chance, I'll put you first. I'll cut my hours back...."

Dimly he heard a soft knock and Vanderford's voice in the outer office.

"I should have talked to you about this a long time ago," he said. "I've hurt you. No matter what else we were to each other, you were my long-time friend. You don't deserve this. I'm sorry," he whispered.

She pulled him close and laid her head on his shoulder. "We were perfect for each other."

"Maybe. But then I met Josie in Paris. I was lonely. I fell hard. I don't know how things will turn out. We've had a rocky start…."

"If it doesn't work out, I'll wait…."

"I can't ask you to do that."

Abigail stroked his cheek. "You don't have to ask."

He was about to tell her no, but a little cry at the door ripped his heart out. The sight of Josie, looking pale and drawn, scared the hell out of him.

"Adam?" Her whisper was strangled.

His heart was hammering wildly as he rushed to Josie. "It's not what you…think."

Josie turned and fled into Vanderford's office. "I—I just came to say goodbye…. When Bob told me you were going, I made him bring me with him. I wanted to surprise you and ride in the car with you out to the airport."

Her face was as white as salt, so white his chest constricted with fresh terror.

"I can explain."

"I'm not asking you to."

Shaking, she stumbled backward. When he ran after her, Vanderford put her arms around Josie and glared daggers at him.

"You were so nice last week. Stupid me…I thought…"

Vanderford glared at him and then spoke gently to Josie.

"Are you all right, Mrs. Ryder? Do you need me to call security? Go down with you?"

"I can take care of my own damn wife, Vanderford!"

"Then I advise you to start doing so, sir."

"It's okay. Bob's waiting for me downstairs. I'll be fine."

Lifting her chin, Josie let go of Vanderford. Turning, she marched down the hall. Adam ran after her. The elevator doors were opening when he grabbed her arm.

"Look, I'm sorry I came and broke up your little…whatever," she said. "I should have known…what was going on all along."

"Nothing is going on."

"I'm not that stupid, Adam."

"I love you," he whispered.

"I saw you. With her. You aren't doing anything wrong. You and she loved each other long before we ever met. We have a deal. A business deal. You'll be a free man in a few months."

"To hell with our business deal! It's always been personal…at least for me. I love you. Why won't you listen to me? I love you."

She pressed a fingertip to his bottom lip. "You don't have to pretend. Not to me. Just let me go."

The bleakness in her tone made his heart tighten. "I don't want to lose you."

"I don't believe you. Not after what I just saw…."

"She told me she loves me. Okay? I felt bad about that, okay? But I love you."

"She was in your arms."

"I don't know how the hell that happened. I guess I was trying to comfort her. Damn it! Why won't you ever listen…or believe me—"

The elevator pinged, and she stepped inside it.

"Go back to her. She's waited so long. Go to Houston. Do your deal. Live your life. We'll stay married in name only…have the baby, and then I'll leave. Just like we agreed. No more repeats of last week's melodrama. Just because you're worried about the baby, you don't have to pretend to feel anything for me."

"Damn it, if you'd ever just listen—"

"You've been generous. I'll ask Bob to call me a taxi when I get downstairs. Don't worry about me. I'll be fine."

Fine. He hated that damned word!

The elevator doors closed, and she's gone.

To his surprise, Abigail was still in his office when he returned.

"I can't go to Houston," he said.

"I'll go," she whispered.

"I love her," he said, clenching his jaw. "How come I didn't know that until our baby nearly died? I hurt you both. Now I may lose her, too. Abigail, I'm sorry about everything."

A single tear slid down her cheek. "I'll be okay, and for what it's worth, I wish you every happiness."

"You're one terrific woman."

"Just go after your wife, okay? She looked pretty broken-up."

Eighteen

Adam's big hands gripped the wheel as he sped through a red light on Congress Avenue. Somebody honked and swerved wildly. He slammed his foot down on the accelerator and raced around the jerk.

He had to get home. He had to make Josie understand that she was the only woman he loved. Somehow he had to talk her in to giving him another chance. If only she would, he'd spend the rest of his life trying to prove to her that he deserved her.

When Adam had grabbed Bob's car keys out of his hand, Bob had given him a sharp look.

"I know. I made her cry. I've got to get home. I need some time alone with Josie to fix that."

"Well, your mother's at the beauty parlor, and I'm due to pick her up in fifteen minutes."

"So, take a taxi. Then keep her busy for an hour or so. Maybe take her to that wildflower center she likes so much. She can't ever set foot in that place without wasting a day."

"What's going on?"

"I need an hour. Maybe two."

"Josie didn't look so hot when she came down. I gave her my number just in case you—"

Adam met his fierce protective glare. "We're on the same side, buddy."

"I used to think so."

"Give us an hour, okay?"

While Beethoven's Fifth Symphony played at top volume, Josie stared wildly at the tangle of gargoyles on her huge canvas. Somehow she'd lost the artistic thread she'd been trying to weave in Paris.

How could she even think about painting when her heart was breaking?

When real life took over, could any artist concentrate? Should they?

All she could see was Abigail's long, slim body coiled tightly against Adam. Despite the symphony, Abigail's soft voice was a constant loop in her head.

I'll put you first. I'll cut my hours back....

Josie's eyes stung. The gargoyles blurred.

Why was it always like this for her? Why was she always on the outside, never able to really fit in, even with those she loved? Why was she never good enough?

She left the painting and ran over to the long windows. Outside the world was bursting with green, which made her think of new life and her baby.

Their baby.

Only slowly did she become aware of Adam in the long shadows of the pecan tree watching her.

Why was he here? What about Houston? Abigail?

Soundlessly, Josie moved toward him. Her hand came up to touch the windowpane. For a long moment she stared into his darkly glittering eyes.

As Beethoven's passionate music built to a crescendo, looking at him suddenly made her long all the more for what she couldn't have. The pain in her heart expanded until she thought her chest would burst.

She began to move rhythmically to the music.

"Watch me," she whispered and then touched the glass again with both hands.

Beads of sweat popped out on his dark forehead. His black hair looked wet and shiny. His expression grim, he ran to the window and raised his hands against the glass where her hands were. No longer the self-contained lawyer, he was tall and powerful and fierce-looking.

With one hand he carelessly loosened his tie and ripped it from his collar. Then with a cry, he jumped toward the door. When he found it locked, he pounded on it and yelled for her to let him in.

She shook her head and began to undulate to the music. Adam's eyes narrowed, and at his fierce look she felt a frisson of sharp desire.

When he leaned down and picked up a rock, she held her breath.

"Unlock the door!"

When she turned her back on him, he threw the rock. Glass shattered, shards tinkling behind her onto the stone floor. He reached inside and unlocked the door.

She turned and met his icy, measuring gaze that slowly ran from the crown of her bright head, down her throat and lush curves, all the way to her long, narrow feet.

With a low growl, he stalked over to the stereo and punched a button that brought instant silence.

"Now…maybe I can hear myself think."

"Is that really why you're here?"

He moved toward her in long, impatient strides.

"What are you doing? Dancing like that when you nearly lost the baby last week? Are you crazy?" he muttered, stopping only when he was mere inches away from her.

"Maybe. Maybe I just wanted your attention."

"Well you damn sure have it. You should be lying down, taking care of yourself…."

"While you play at the office with pretty Abigail."

"I don't want her. I want you. Most of all I want you to take better care of yourself."

"You mean that I should be taking care of the baby?"

"No, you little fool." With a single fingertip he touched her damp cheek. "You've been crying…. Josie, please listen to me." He pulled out his handkerchief and dried her cheeks with it. "I'm not just concerned about the baby. *I love you.* I told Abigail I love you. I should have told her before, but I told her today, and she believes me. She accepts that whatever we had in the past is over. So, now, you and I really do have to talk. About us. I want us to have a real marriage. I always have."

"You really…mean that?"

"Yes."

When Josie just stood very still, not yet knowing whether to believe him or not, he moved even closer.

When his gaze fell to her flushed, moist lips, she licked them and then drew in a quick, uncertain breath. Then his powerful arms slid around her, and he pulled her against his chest.

"I love you," he said again.

"Do you? Can that really be possible?"

"Yes, damn it, yes!"

She shivered in elemental awareness of him.

"Do you?" Her hands climbed his chest. "Do you?" Tentatively her fingertips stroked his hard cheek and then his mouth. Finally, she stretched onto her tiptoes and circled his neck with her arms.

"Yes, I do. I love you," he said as he wrapped his arms around her tightly, pulling her against his body.

For a long moment Josie didn't hear anything but the thunder of her own heart beating in unison with his.

"I love you," he said huskily.

She breathed in the words, almost believing them.

Then his mouth found hers, and his tongue invaded her lips, and it was like that first night when she'd felt they'd always been lovers. It was as if he crawled into her skin, and they were one. Again, she knew what she'd known that night, that he was the only one for her. Maybe, maybe he knew it, too.

"We have to talk," he said. "I have to make you believe…."

Her body was stretched so tautly against his, his fiery heat consumed her. Maybe she did believe him.

"Talk? But do we? What if I already do believe you? What if I have another idea?"

"But do you believe me?"

"Do you think you always get to control everything we do? Every feeling we have?"

"Shouldn't you be lying down?" he said. "Resting?"

"Good idea." She ran her hand down his chest and then

pulled him gently toward the low sofa he'd ordered Bob to move to her studio.

"No sex," he said. "We can't risk—"

"Maybe you're not in charge tonight."

"Why did you marry me?" he whispered.

"Not because of the money. Or the baby. Because I wanted to. Because…"

"Why? Say it. Maybe I have to hear it, too."

"Because I love you."

"Finally. So, you're not going to leave me after the baby is born. You're going to stay here, always, with me."

He caught her mouth with his, drinking in her taste deeply. She held on tight with her arms and legs and kissed him back.

"We can't have sex," he said.

"Which means we'll have to use our imagination. And that's what artists are good at. We can do other things…. Incredible things." She smiled shyly. "I have an idea that has to do with a girl standing in a window while a stranger watches. When she excites him past the point of no return, she can…"

She leaned over him and whispered the rest of her fantasy in his ear. When she sat up and began to unbutton her shirt, she saw that his eyes were already glittering darkly with desire.

"See—aren't you glad you married me?"

"Oh, yes…yes…yes…."

When she removed her blouse and bra, he traced the soft shape of her breasts, teasing her nipples with hands that shook.

"Not yet," she murmured. "You have to go outside and watch me undress first."

"Not until you kiss me again and tell me you love me."

"I love you. Always and forever."

"You forgot to kiss me."

"I was saving the best part for last."

When she opened her mouth, his tongue filled hers. He pressed his mouth closer and closer, until she felt the warmth of his love in every cell in her being.

She was loved. At last.

The man at her window was no longer a stranger. He was her husband, and the father of her precious son.

"Oh, Adam, I don't deserve to be this happy."

"That's where you're wrong. Where you've always been wrong. You're a beautiful, sensitive woman, who deserves to be loved and admired and cherished. Maybe it's time we both lightened up on ourselves."

He caught her mouth in another all-consuming kiss that went on and on for a very long time.

Epilogue

Christmas, one year later
Austin, Texas

Josie squeezed Adam's hand as they stood together in the yellow nursery staring down at their black-headed son, who was dark and long-bodied and the spitting image of his father, or so everybody said.

"Jake looks so cute curled up in that red velvet onesy your mom got him," Josie said. "I can't believe he won't wake up for Christmas."

"Next year when he's all over the place, we'll be wishing he'd take a nap."

"Don't you think he gets cuter every day?" Josie asked.

"And tougher, too," Adam murmured.

"Like his daddy."

"We'll have to get him a pair of boots and a Stetson soon. We'll have him on a horse before he can walk."

"Not alone, I hope," Josie said.

"No, he'll be with me."

Downstairs Marion was laughing at something outrageous Gigi had said.

As she listened to their mothers, who got along amazingly well, Josie held her breath. She couldn't believe that she was finally having the Christmas she'd always dreamed of, with real presents piled high under a real Christmas tree. But she was.

The house was decorated to the max and filled with Christmas guests, including Lucas and Marion and Camille Vanderford, as well as all of Josie's family from New Orleans.

Bob had a turkey in the oven, and the scent of rosemary and thyme and turkey meat drifted up the stairs. "The Night Before Christmas" was playing in every room, and a three-story tree that had taken Bob a week to erect and decorate stood in their living room.

"This is the best Christmas ever," Josie said. "At least for me."

"For me, too, because I have you…and Jake."

"Family," Josie whispered. Finally, because of Adam, she felt that she belonged to a real family.

Adam pulled her close and brushed her cheek with his lips, maybe to dispel even the shadow of a doubt.

"Merry Christmas," he whispered.

"The merriest ever. At least for me," she said.

"For me, too. What would my life be without you?"

"Or mine? I never thought that such happiness was possible."

"When Jake's a little older, we'll get Mother to come stay a few days. I'll take you back to Paris for a delayed honeymoon."

"Maybe we can rent the same apartments…. Or one with a view of the Eiffel Tower…."

"And I can watch you from the dark…."

"We can do that here…tonight," she said.

She slipped into his arms, and he kissed her long and hard until Jake began to whimper. Then they picked him up, cuddled him close and kissed and hugged him, too.

* * * * *

SPECIAL EDITION®

Life, Love and Family

*These contemporary romances will strike a chord
with you as heroines juggle life
and relationships on their way to true love.*

New York Times *bestselling author Linda Lael Miller
brings you a BRAND-NEW contemporary story
featuring her fan-favorite McKettrick family.*

Meg McKettrick is surprised to be reunited with her high
school flame, Brad O'Ballivan. After enjoying a career
as a country-and-western singer, Brad aches for a home
and family…and seeing Meg again makes him realize he
still loves her. But their pride manages to interfere with
love…until an unexpected matchmaker gets involved.

*Turn the page for a sneak preview of
THE McKETTRICK WAY
by Linda Lael Miller
On sale November 20,
wherever books are sold.*

Brad shoved the truck into gear and drove to the bottom of the hill, where the road forked. Turn left, and he'd be home in five minutes. Turn right, and he was headed for Indian Rock.

He had no damn business going to Indian Rock.

He had nothing to say to Meg McKettrick, and if he never set eyes on the woman again, it would be two weeks too soon.

He turned right.

He couldn't have said why.

He just drove straight to the Dixie Dog Drive-In.

Back in the day, he and Meg used to meet at the Dixie Dog, by tacit agreement, when either of them had been away. It had been some kind of universe thing, purely intuitive.

Passing familiar landmarks, Brad told himself he ought to turn around. The old days were gone. Things had ended badly between him and Meg anyhow, and she wasn't going to be at the Dixie Dog.

He kept driving.

He rounded a bend, and there was the Dixie Dog. Its big neon sign, a giant hot dog, was all lit up and going through its corny sequence—first it was covered in red squiggles of light, meant to suggest ketchup, and then yellow, for mustard.

Brad pulled into one of the slots next to a speaker, rolled down the truck window and ordered.

A girl roller-skated out with the order about five minutes later.

When she wheeled up to the driver's window, smiling, her eyes went wide with recognition, and she dropped the tray with a clatter.

Silently Brad swore. Damn if he hadn't forgotten he was a famous country singer.

The girl, a skinny thing wearing too much eye makeup, immediately started to cry. "I'm sorry!" she sobbed, squatting to gather up the mess.

"It's okay," Brad answered quietly, leaning to look down at her, catching a glimpse of her plastic name tag. "It's okay, Mandy. No harm done."

"I'll get you another dog and a shake right away, Mr. O'Ballivan!"

"Mandy?"

She stared up at him pitifully, sniffling. Thanks to the copious tears, most of the goop on her eyes had slid south. "Yes?"

"When you go back inside, could you not mention seeing me?"

"But you're Brad O'Ballivan!"

"Yeah," he answered, suppressing a sigh. "I know."

She rolled a little closer. "You wouldn't happen to have a picture you could autograph for me, would you?"

"Not with me," Brad answered.

"You could sign this napkin, though," Mandy said. "It's only got a little chocolate on the corner."

Brad took the paper napkin and her order pen, and scrawled his name. Handed both items back through the window.

She turned and whizzed back toward the side entrance to the Dixie Dog.

Brad waited, marveling that he hadn't considered incidents like this one before he'd decided to come back home. In retrospect, it seemed shortsighted, to say the least, but the truth was, he'd expected to be—Brad O'Ballivan.

Presently Mandy skated back out again, and this time she managed to hold on to the tray.

"I didn't tell a soul!" she whispered. "But Heather and Darlene *both* asked me why my mascara was all smeared." Efficiently she hooked the tray onto the bottom edge of the window.

Brad extended payment, but Mandy shook her head.

"The boss said it's on the house, since I dumped your first order on the ground."

He smiled. "Okay, then. Thanks."

Mandy retreated, and Brad was just reaching for the food when a bright red Blazer whipped into the space beside his. The driver's door sprang open, crashing into the metal speaker, and somebody got out in a hurry.

Something quickened inside Brad.

And in the next moment Meg McKettrick was standing practically on his running board, her blue eyes blazing.

Brad grinned. "I guess you're not over me after all," he said.

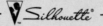

SPECIAL EDITION™

brings you a heartwarming
new McKettrick's story from

NEW YORK TIMES BESTSELLING AUTHOR

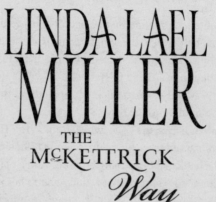

LINDA LAEL MILLER

THE McKETTRICK *Way*

Meg McKettrick is surprised to be reunited
with her high school flame, Brad O'Ballivan,
who has returned home to his family's
neighboring ranch. After seeing Meg again,
Brad realizes he still loves her. But the pride
of both manage to interfere with love...until
an unexpected matchmaker gets involved.

—— McKettrick Women ——

Available December wherever you buy books.

REQUEST YOUR FREE BOOKS!

2 FREE NOVELS PLUS 2 FREE GIFTS!

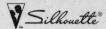

Passionate, Powerful, Provocative!

COMING NEXT MONTH

#1837 THE EXECUTIVE'S SURPRISE BABY—
Catherine Mann
The Garrisons
The news of his impending fatherhood was shocking…
discovering the mother of his baby didn't want to marry him—
unbelievable.

#1838 SPENCER'S FORBIDDEN PASSION—
Brenda Jackson
A Westmoreland bachelor got more than he bargained for when
he turned his hostile takeover bid into a marriage-of-convenience
offer.

#1839 RICH MAN'S VENGEFUL SEDUCTION—
Laura Wright
No Ring Required
He had one goal: seduce the woman who left him years ago and
leave her cold. Could he carry out his plan after a night together
ignites old passions?

#1840 MARRIED OR NOT?—Annette Broadrick
The last person she needed or wanted to see was her
ex-husband…until she discovered they could still be man and
wife.

#1841 HIS STYLE OF SEDUCTION—Roxanne St. Claire
She was charged with giving this millionaire a makeover. But she
was the one in for a big change...in the bedroom.

#1842 THE MAGNATE'S MARRIAGE DEMAND—
Robyn Grady
A wealthy tycoon demanded the woman pregnant with the heir
to his family dynasty marry him. But their passionate union was
anything but all business.